To Avril

Hoping you still
enjoy the stay!

J J

nune

THE INCEPTOR TRILOGY
VOLUME 3
QUATRAIN 77

By the same author:

*The Inceptor Trilogy Volume 1 –
The Spirit*, The Book Guild, 2006

*The Inceptor Trilogy Volume 2 –
The Patient*, The Book Guild, 2007

THE INCEPTOR TRILOGY
VOLUME 3
QUATRAIN 77

Maureen Farenden

Book Guild Publishing
Sussex, England

First published in Great Britain in 2007 by
The Book Guild Ltd
Pavilion View
19 New Road
Brighton, BN1 1UF

Typesetting in Baskerville by
Keyboard Services, Luton, Bedfordshire

Printed in Great Britain by
CPI Bath

A catalogue record for this book is available from
The British Library

ISBN 978 1 84624 128 4

Contents

1

The Gates

Darkness is almost upon her as the gates of the underworld open, beckoning her to enter, as Lucifer drains the life force from her.

'Look into the gates of hell, Charity, and know your destiny. Come give yourself to me and know the true power of Satan.'

Her mind is swirling in a pit of despair. Her gift is powerless, as Lucifer carries her down into his world. She hears the cries of eternal damnation, but still she cannot betray her Lord or her charge. How has she come to this? There is no way out...

'There must be another way? Please, my Lord, show me the way,' she cries.

The Lord of Darkness crushes her spirit within his huge bat wings and feels her soul becoming his. He laughs aloud, confident that victory, at last, will be his, as he feels her will ebbing away. Her time is up and she succumbs, unable to choose, sealing her destiny... Her body is almost a shell as despair slips into emptiness. Forsaken by her Lord and betrayed by her own family whose dark secret has entombed her in its pestilence.

'Where are my heaven-sent powers now? Forsaken and lost. Is this to be my fate? I weep. I cry. Yet no one comes.' Too weak to speak, her words are but silent thoughts, as the gates open wider, waiting. Her mind wanders, as Lucifer's powers take hold, and his will becomes hers. She thinks of Monty.

'I can see his strong face and gentle smile and feel the warmth of his love. Oh, how I shall miss his strength. He would be better off without me, for I bring him such pain and darkness. The constant battles that tear at his soul, draining his strength, now he will know peace. He will love again. I must free him of this terrible burden … me.'

Her thoughts grow darker.

'My dear Robyn, she's so young and beautiful and I bring her the despair of lost souls.'

Her spirit and soul is almost his, as her last thoughts turn to the RING.

'How cruel I have been to drag them into my world, I must release them. Let them know peace and not fear. For a while, they will miss me, but soon their lives will be safer. They will survive without me. This I know.'

Her body, almost transparent with hopelessness, floats towards her fate. She is at the gates, looking into the jaws of the underworld. Lucifer's words resounding through her.

'Look beyond the gates, Charity, and see what welcomes you into my kingdom.'

She can barely focus, the tears blinding her, as she rubs her eyes and sees a distant figure. It is calling to her, she wipes away the tears to see … a miracle…

2

The Sorceress

She stares into the fires of hell, aghast at what she sees...
Annie! Her beloved sister, floating in the distance, her
arms stretched out, beckoning her into them. Her long,
silky black hair flowing widely in the flames of hell, her
luminous face mesmerising her with its haunting beauty.

'Is it really she? Or is this a cruel illusion?'

Charity's strength returns, and as she draws closer, her
beloved sister's smile grows ever more bewitching. She is
so beautiful. Robyn is indeed the reincarnation of her
mother. How she wishes she could see her now.

Just as they become one, and Charity is about to be
enveloped in her arms, she hears a soft voice whispering
to her.

'I am here, my daughter. My Lord has sent me to you
through the power of infallible thought. Listen to my
voice, Charity, it is sent by divine intervention.'

Charity freezes. She feels Ma's spirit entering her,
holding her back, as Annie calls to her.

'Sister, dear sister, I have longed to feel your love again.
Come to me, Charity. Let me show you the pleasures of
my Lord's kingdom. Join me, dear sister, and revel in his
glory.'

Her voice is that of an angel, caressing her with its
silky promises of eternal happiness.

3

'You must not listen to her, my daughter. Her words are fallacious. Look beyond the illusion and see the reality. Feel the power of the angels flow within you.'

Ma's protective words dull the luminous light of her sister, as Charity's gift is reborn, bringing forth her power of 'clear seeing'. The vision of beguiling beauty before her shape-shifts into half woman, half bird. Two heads that sit upon the body of a woman. The crow and the female, bound together as one. The hands of a woman and the feet of a crow dressed in robes of green and red with vines of thorns flowing from her, which twist and turn in the air like serpents. She holds the apple of forbidden fruit in her right hand and the sceptre of Lucifer in her left. She is the gatekeeper of the underworld.

Charity's blood runs cold, as illusion becomes reality, and she is face to face with the Devil's darkest disciple, the queen of black witches, the Sorceress. Created by Lucifer from the warm blood of dead crows and women, she casts her spells of evil upon all that she encounters. The ancient *Book of Shadows* tells of her despicable crimes against humanity and her unquenchable thirst for the blood of innocents.

Charity knows of this powerful black witch from this ancient book, shown to her in a secret coven by a white witch, which contains the secrets of Wicca, also known as witchcraft. Legend has it that those who have the gift of Wicca in their souls will inherit its powerful magic, which has been passed down through centuries to the chosen ones whose powers are indelibly written in blood in this ancient book of spells. Both white and black witches covet this book, which offers infinite powers to the holder of the spells contained within it. Its shamanic magic was first derived from the Druids, who had the mystical powers of shape-shifting. Over the centuries, the followers of shamanism and the Druid ways wrote all the secrets in the form of spells, which became the bible of Wicca. This secret bible has the power to bring forth the light and dark side of the spirit world and give the custodian the ability of shape-shifting.

'Do not fear me, Charity, for I bring you your sister's love, which is waiting for you. Come with me, Charity, and know who you really are.'

She knows this devil witch is evil incarnate, but still she finds herself drifting into her arms, which, for a moment, look like Annie's, as she loses herself in their soft embrace.

Then the pain begins. She opens her eyes to find herself entwined within the Sorceress's vines, as the thorns cut into her flesh, drawing blood. Slowly, she feels the life force draining from her, her blood trickling into the thorns and along the vines until it reaches the Sorceress's two heads. The crow dips its black beak into Charity's warm blood and then turns to feed its partner, the Sorceress.

Charity watches as the two of them gorge on her blood, the vines gripping tighter and tighter, until there is no escape. She can hear a faint voice calling to her, but she is weak and unable to respond, as time begins to run out.

'Beloved sister, hear me now, see the *Book of Shadows* and cast the spell of Wicca. I come to you through the spirits of the Druid underworld. Listen to me, dear sister, and know the power of Wicca, which is inherent in us both. Feel the magic within your soul and free us both. Hurry, Charity, hurry.'

Annie's voice is that of a tortured spirit reaching out, yet Charity's gift tells her that there are two souls within her. She feels the warmth of a sister's protective love, but there is another creature, which is dark and malevolent. This evil spirit controls both souls, imprisoning Annie in the dark underworld.

5

What does Annie mean by the spirits of the Druid underworld, and the power of Wicca inherent in them both? 'I'm not a witch,' she thinks to herself. 'I have the power of the angels within me. I am an inceptor, with the gift of clear seeing. I know nothing of spells and the practice of magic, black or white. Is this really Annie's voice calling to me, or another trick?'

Her head is spinning in a whirl of tortured doubts, her body slowly ravaged by the crow and the witch, sinking deeper and deeper into the fires of hell, unable to help the lost spirit of Polly or herself.

She sinks down into the darkness, carried by the vines of the Sorceress, as Annie cries out to her. 'See the *Book of Shadows*, Charity, and cast the spell of Wicca. Hear the whispers of your ancestors, the Druid spirits, and become as they. Listen to them calling to you from the darkness where they have been waiting for this time. Listen and know who you are. Feel the power of Wicca and release its magic. Look into the book of spells. Look, Charity, look.'

She closes her eyes and begins to see, as the pages turn, and the spirits whisper.

'See the spell of DAW, Charity. Read its words to invoke its powers and call upon its magic.'

The pages stop turning, as the book floats before her, and the spirits whisper.

'Call upon its magic, Charity, and become who you are.'

She reads the spell.

'I cast the binding spell of DAW to bring forth the third element
Dragon's blood – to bring the power of spells to life.
Asafoetida – the disposer of evil.
Wormwood – the bringer of protection.

I offer these three herbs to the king of water, Zephyrus,
to beseech him to come into me and bring forth the gods
of the third element.'

The spell is cast and the book closes, as Charity feels the spirit of Zephyrus within her, speaking in the tongue of shamanic verse.

'Feel the pure energy of my elemental form within you, Charity, and use the power of the third element, water, to release you and your charge. Become water. Flow like water. Be water. Become the vessel into which you flow. Be the vessel. Call upon the gods and let the waters run...'

3

Power of the Shape-Shifter

A huge torrent of water rises up from beneath the darkness, engulfing all that it touches, breaking the Sorceress's vines and releasing Charity. She sees the crow and witch swallowed up, swept away in a tidal wave, the crow torn from the witch, hearing their screams of terror, as they drown in the mighty waters of the Gods.

She can feel herself submerging, the waters immersing her body in one gigantic deluge, plunging her down into the icy cold darkness. She catches her breath, as the water pours through her mouth into her body, filling her up, until she succumbs, and the shadow of death touches her. Her body becomes weightless and shapeless in the flowing water, which becomes a living lagoon, as she drifts in the clear, cold lake.

Just at the moment of expiration, she hears the call of the gods.

'Soak in the life of the living lagoon, Charity, and become it. Feel the power of running water, which keeps on flowing and never dies. Swallow its purity and drink in its energy. Become the source of its power. Look into the lagoon, Charity, and see.'

She opens her eyes and sees a beautiful lagoon, protected by tall green trees, growing out of rocks and sandy beaches covered in seashells. She is floating in the calm, blue waters that are caressing her body, the life force raging through her. An overwhelming feeling of power and energy charges through her, as she rises out of the lagoon into the air. There is something different about her.

She is flying like a bird, but still feels like a woman.

She looks down into the lagoon and sees the waters rising up towards her, a wave, which becomes the face of a beautiful woman, the goddess of the lagoon.

'I awaken your powers, Charity. Look within and feel the call of your ancestors. I give you back what is yours, as decreed by the sacred Druids. Use your powers wisely, Charity, for the time is coming. I give back to you the power of the four elements: air, fire, water and earth, the four energies that form the magic of the shape-shifter. Go now, and fulfil your destiny.'

Suddenly she sees her reflection in the waters, and what she sees horrifies, yet comforts her, at the same time. She is part woman, part sea eagle. Her head and arms are moulded into the body of a great sea eagle, which carries her through the air. Its magnificent brown and white feathers spread wide, as it weaves its way upwards, while droplets of water fall down into the disappearing lagoon. Swifter and swifter she flies, as she feels the power of the eagle beneath her, her heart pounding and her blood racing, the life force within her growing more powerful by the second. She has never felt more courageous or invincible. Nothing or no one can stop her, as the sea eagle-woman flies upwards, through the fires of hell, faster than the speed of light, emerging from the deadly embrace of Lucifer's wings.

The court is aghast, as she flies valiantly above them, her wings so vast that they cover all that is beneath them.

'Holy mother of God, what is this abomination?' cries Lizzy

The others look up, horrified, but relieved that their

9

beloved Charity is free. What is this creature floating above them, magnificent in its ugliness? Is it really her? Suddenly it swoops down, hovering over Monty, their eyes locked, as he gazes in tortured disbelief at the two-headed monster before him.

'Spud, is that really you?' he asks, terrified of his own wife.

She smiles, as the eagle screeches, two spirits joined as one. Even when the beast is within her, Monty crumbles. Darkness descends upon the court, swallowing it up in the vileness of Lucifer's presence.

'So you have been reprieved by the power of the shape-shifter's magic,' he rages.

Flying high above them, suspended, his great bat wings overshadowing all, he swishes his mighty tail back and forth, menacingly.

He laughs, aloud, as the angels look on, floating above their throne, their swords wielded and ready for combat.

Charity turns, looking to her angels and then Lucifer, who waits, eager for battle, confident that his dark powers will win. The RING is motionless, frozen with fear, as they struggle to find a way out of this continuing nightmare.

The sea eagle-woman spreads her wings, feeling the power of the shape-shifter within her, as she looks down at Monty. 'Believe in me, believe in us. Trust me. I am still the Inceptor. Protect the others.'

They smile at each other, that knowing, silent smile of theirs that says everything. She turns to face Lucifer. 'I choose the third choice, freedom.'

He looks down upon her, his Satanic eyes penetrating her whole being. 'Freedom comes at a price, Charity, are you willing to risk all these souls to save just two? Surrender now and I will take only what is due, Polly and you.'

For a moment, she falters, as she looks down upon Monty and her family, but the power of the shape-shifter

10

flows within her, which grows more prevalent by the second.

'Without freedom there is nothing, why offer to take only two when you know that eventually you will have all, if freedom is no longer theirs to command? You offer an empty choice.'

He flexes his wings, ready for flight, his depraved laugh reverberating throughout the court. 'Brave words, Charity, but empty ones against my power.' He folds his huge wings behind him, suspending the full ugliness of the beast for all to see, half man, half devil, horned, tailed, and ready for battle. He speaks the words of Beelzebub, as his wings unfold, summoning his familiars of the underworld to do his bidding.

The cobra, a spectacular 60-foot cobra-woman, slithers out from its master's protective wings, uncoiling, floating above them, a she-devil's head upon the cobra's powerful, scaly green body. Once you feel the embrace of this deadly familiar, life is crushed from you, when the she-devil becomes the cobra and swallows its prey whole.

The wolfhound, part woman, part wolf, emerges from Lucifer's dark underworld to reveal a bloodthirsty creature that exists only to kill. A black she-wolf of immense power and strength, upon which sits two heads, the wolf and the black witch of the underworld. The two are joined, side by side, the witch commanding the wolf whose powerful jaws are always open, its long, pointed sabre teeth dripping with saliva, impatient for its next meal. This she-wolf will tear at your flesh with its claws, as the witch revels in your screams of pain before, finally, devouring you with its mighty jaws. It is a slow, agonizing death.

Finally he appears; the sea serpent, the devil serpent of the sea and the bringer of the eternal waters of death. A wondrous, sleek, muscular man, whose body is the

11

perfection of the gods, which flows into a serpent's tail, his handsome face captivating all who gaze upon it. His dark hair, streaked with gold, flows like a warrior's mane down his back, but beware! This Adonis of the sea has a dark, treacherous nature. Up close, his seductive face shape-shifts into a blood-curdling green sea monster, who, with one bite, rips the head off its victims, condemning them to an eternity of floating in a river of blood; their own.

The cobra, wolfhound and sea serpent, the devil's three demon familiars of the underworld, eagerly await the command of their master, hungry for the taste of fresh blood.

The RING stare in silence, quaking in trepidation, knowing that their feeble bodies are useless against these unholy creatures.

Charity knows this and must call upon the magic of Wicca to invoke its powers, if she is to win their freedom. Swiftly the sea eagle-woman calls to her angels.

'Mighty angels of my Lord, send to me the instrument that will form the circle of invocation, bringing forth the power of the one true being.'

Instantly, the Angel of Justice raises his left arm high behind him, and with one mighty thrust, throws his scales of justice into the air, sending them somersaulting towards Charity, who spreads her magnificent wings, flying towards them, as she catches, not scales, but an athame. The scales have transformed into a white handled knife, a white witch's athame, used to draw a protective circle around its master and servants. The holder of it has the power to create hybrid creatures within the circle, which have the power of the angels within them.

In the blink of an eye, Charity flies towards the RING, drawing a circle around them with the athame, protecting them, as Lucifer commands his demon familiars to wreak havoc. They come with all the force of a demonic army, as Charity and the RING await their fate inside the circle. She calls to her angels.

'Protect the circle, so that I may bring forth the power of the athame.'

The mighty angels spread their wings, raising their swords, as the Angel of Judgment blows his horn, summoning the powers of heaven, as the battle commences.

They swoop down, intercepting Lucifer's demon creatures. Charity calls upon the magic of the athame. The Devil watches, suspended on his throne of power, as his creatures rage into battle.

The cobra entwines her scaly body around Justice, trapping his wings, cutting off his ability to fly, crushing the spirit from him, feeling his bones crumble, while he desperately tries to strike through her monstrous head with his sword. Its grip is too strong, as his bones crack and wings break, while the cobra gets ready to strike.

To the right, Judgment is fighting the wolfhound, as the sea serpent floats nearby, waiting for his time. God's mighty angel feels the excruciating pain of the she-wolf's claws penetrating his skin, drawing blood, as the black witch whispers her spells of death into the wolf's ears. The she-wolf tears into Judgment's wings, ripping them to shreds, as he struggles to maintain flight. His sword falls from his hand, down into the fires of hell, while Lucifer watches, soaking in every dark moment of pleasure, as he sees Charity's angels crumbling before him.

In the circle, the RING watch, helpless, as their valiant protectors fight to the death.

'They are losing, Charity, it is hopeless. We are doomed,' cries Robyn. Her heart beats so fast that she can barely breathe, while the others pray for a miracle.

'God help us from these vile creatures,' shouts Monty. Charity raises the athame in the air, while reciting the

13

words of the deity, the custodian of the magic knife, and the only one who has the power to evoke its magic.

'I am she, who commands the athame, whose touch takes on the shapes of beasts upon men. Accept my rule and let the beast be filled and my bidding be done.'

She bends down, touching Monty, Jack and Robyn with the tip of the knife, as their bodies mutate into animal hybrids. Monty transforms into the falcon-man, half man, half bird of prey. Magnificent brown-feathered wings grow from his back, as his feet turn inwards, becoming deadly claws. His body and arms take on the physique of a warrior, while his head metamorphoses into the falcon. In his right hand he holds the sword of ending, which brings swift death to all that it touches.

Jack mutates into the lion-man, half man, half lion, as his glorious muscular upper body grows from the back of his magnificent shaggy mane. The lion's powerful jaws and claws can destroy any enemy in seconds, while Jack, the soldier, commands the beast.

Lastly, Robyn, the three-headed dolphin, whose sleek body swims effortlessly through the spiritual waters of the air. Robyn's head is in the centre showing them the way, while the other two dolphins penetrate their enemy's eardrums, their silent screeches exploding their brains; killing them instantly.

Lizzy, Sam and Leo cannot believe their eyes, as they watch, transfixed by these supernatural beasts.

'We are in a nightmare and there is no escape,' yells Leo, clutching Sam tightly, their bodies trembling uncontrollably.

Lizzy, for once, is lost for words, as she kneels down clutching her rosary beads and praying like never before.

Suddenly they hear a cry, turning to see the cobra coiling her venomous body around Justice, tightening like a vice, squeezing the life force from him, until his body

14

snaps into two. She raises her hooded head, until they are eye-to-eye, the she-devil looking into the soul of this courageous angel. She turns to her master, who signals his end, as she swings her head around, opening her mouth, swallowing his broken body, whole.

As the cobra digests her meal, the wolfhound prepares to follow suit, commanded by the witch, who casts her final spell upon the ravaged and bloody body of Judgment. The wolfhound awaits its master's command, as the sea serpent moves closer, floating like a shimmering god. Lucifer laughs, revelling in the demise of these majestic creatures, holy protectors of a Lord who was once his master, but whose souls he now possesses.

'Where is your mighty Lord now? You spend centuries guarding His kingdom, only to be forsaken. Breathe your last breath of light, for darkness is your master now.'

The wolfhound savours the final pieces of flesh, as Judgment's screams reverberate through the air, while the sea serpent slides closer, his handsome face glowing with light, when, suddenly, it transforms into an ugly snarling sea monster, its teeth ripping Judgment's head off his shoulders, leaving his headless body floating in a pool of his own blood. Down and down he falls, swimming in his own blood, into the underworld...

Charity and the RING watch, shocked to the very core of their souls, as these beautiful mystical creatures are lost to the dark underworld for all time. If these mighty angels cannot defeat Lucifer's beasts, then what chance have they?

The circle breaks, as Lucifer's dark powers destroy the magic of the athame, freeing his familiars, who rage at the RING, hungry for more.

Charity commands her army, sending them into battle. Robyn swims swiftly through the air towards Lucifer, as the three dolphins weave their way in and around him,

15

their high-pitched screeches penetrating his ears, disabling him, as he fights to regain his powers.

The lion-man leaps at the devil sea serpent, his claws ripping into its body, tearing at its flesh, as Jack grabs its ugly head in his powerful arms, pulling its jaws apart, fighting ferociously in the air, as their bodies twist and turn. The lion claws and scratches at the serpent's sleek body, until it's just bone and blood, while Jack, the demon soldier, rips its jaws apart with his bare hands, his powerful muscles pulsating. With one final bite from the lion's mighty jaws, the devil's serpent is no more, as his mangled body falls from the air.

Jack looks around to see Monty and the she-wolf flying through the air, as the falcon-man spreads his magnificent wings, picking the wolfhound up with his claws. The witch casts her spell, destroying the falcon's claws, releasing her from their grip. The wolf leaps at Monty, sinking its blood-curdling teeth into the falcon's neck, drawing blood, while the witch empowers its grip with her black magic. Monty feels the life force draining from him.

Jack leaps to his rescue, pouncing on the wolf, sinking his powerful jaws into its body, as it howls in agonising pain. The two spin through the air, ripping into each other, the beasts commanded by Jack and Monty. The witch casts her spell, but Monty is too quick, as he raises his right hand, cutting her head clean off with his sword, destroying them.

They are weak from loss of blood, as they see the cobra's venomous body coiled around Charity, crushing her. She looks to them, as the cobra faces up to her, spreading her gigantic hooded head wide, ready for the kill.

The power of the warrior rages through Monty, who thrusts his sword through the air, stabbing the cobra, loosening her grip, as the sea eagle flies at her. The power of Wicca races through Charity, empowering her with its magic. Charity looks down upon the bloody and beaten cobra, which, as she uncoils, looks to her master for help. She struggles to release herself from Monty's sword of ending, which, once inside, remains, until every drop of blood has been drained. The master cannot help her, as he battles to rid his head from the deadly sounds of the dolphins, which swim, effortlessly, through the air, in and around him, screeching, exploding his grotesque goat's head with their incessant sounds. He is paralysed, unable to think, shaking his head violently, his dark powers useless against the sound of the spirit dolphins.

Charity seizes the chance. She whispers to the sea eagle, which swoops in and around her prey, sizing her up, as the cobra hisses and spits, trying to catch this magnificent bird in its jaws. Her powers grow weaker, as Charity's grow stronger. Round and round the sea eagle flies, swifter and swifter it swoops, commanded by its master, Charity, wearing the cobra down, until it no longer has the strength to fight. The cobra-woman raises her hooded head up for the last time, as the sea eagle looks down upon her, two great beasts of the gods, the dark and light, going into final battle. The eagle screeches its cry of victory, swooping down upon the she-devil's head, plucking her eyes out with its deadly beak, as she recoils in agony, succumbing to the call of death.

Lucifer's three demon beasts are destroyed by the RING, who come together, forming the circle of victory, Sam, Lizzy and Leo, side by side, with their victorious shape-shifting beasts. The power of the RING has never been as formidable as this moment, as they look straight into the eyes of Lucifer.

'Release Polly, or hear the sounds of the dolphins for all eternity,' Charity commands.

'You would condemn your family into hell in order to save one pathetic soul?'

'I have the power of infallible thought, which, together with the magic of Wicca, will put the sound of the spirit dolphins in your thoughts, the never ending screeching, which will tear away at you. You will never die from it like a mere mortal or one of your demons, but you will never feel the peace of silence either. Is the soul of Polly worth such torture?'

They stare each other down, the Inceptor and the Lord of Darkness; both filled with such hate and rage that neither can see beyond the moment. He can wait. He has already waited longer than the creation of man, so for now, he concedes.

'This is not the definitive battle, Charity. Your path was set before you were born. You cannot avoid your destiny. The beginning of the end has just begun...'

He folds his huge bat wings around him, as darkness overshadows all, and the RING spiral into an empty void of blackness.

4

Lady of the Shadows

Charity feels the ground beneath her. She looks down to discover she is back. The beast has gone, as the RING regain their mortal bodies.

'I'll never complain about the size of my bum again,' says Robyn, looking around for a mirror, desperate, yet terrified to see her reflection.

'Hang on a minute; I know this place. Shit we are back in the hospital again,' cries Sam.

Leo looks at her, shocked, he has never heard her swear.

'Can't a girl express her feelings?' she says, ashamed.

Charity senses that there is something else in the ward, which is not of this world. She looks around; they are back in the present, in the exact same spot where she first encountered Polly's spirit. She looks over at the bed in the corner, Polly's bed, where an old man is sleeping. The ward is dark, with just a glimmer of light flickering through the doors from the hallway, as the patients sleep, and the night nurse is outside, grabbing a quick smoke.

Then it appears...

A ghostly silhouette rises out of the old man's body, floating towards them, smiling. Charity knows this spirit, and as it draws closer, she feels its soul touch hers. A

19

beautiful young woman, with long dark flowing hair stands before her.

'Thank you, my dear, thank you,' she says softly.

Suddenly the room changes, they are in a cemetery, walking towards a gravestone through the icy mist of the night.

'Look at the stone, Charity, look.'

'I cannot see anything, it's blank.'

'Look again, look into its soul.'

'I see, I see.'

Her heart leaps, as the stone comes alive, and the words 'Polly Melrose, may her soul rest in peace' are inscribed upon it.

'You gave me back my name, Charity, so I give you back yours.'

'But I have a name,' she replies, puzzled, yet afraid at the same time.

'You have one more final quest to make, which will take you to the edge of the antediluvian world, where you will discover the truth of who you are.'

'But I know who I am; I'm Charity Holmes, the Inceptor.'

Polly moves closer, touching her face with her translucent hand, as the two melt into one. Charity sees the shadow of a woman in the darkness, imprisoned by the invisible bars of the underworld. She knows this woman, yet does not. She has no soul. She is a vacant shell. She exists only in the shadows, where time is limitless.

'I do not understand. Who is this woman and what is she to me? Why do you want to give me back something I already possess?' she asks, her voice trembling with fear, the fear of discovery.

'Go back, Charity; go back to the beginning, where the end is the beginning. Look to your sister, Annie. Look to your mother. Look to your family. Hear the call of your ancestors and know who you are. Know your name, Charity. Know your destiny.'

'Stop, stop, I have had enough,' she cries, holding her head in her hands.

Monty reaches out to comfort her. Suddenly everything goes blank, as her legs turn to jelly and her body drifts away. The light goes out, as darkness descends, and the sleep of emptiness creeps over her...

5

The Witch's Tale

She awakes. The room is spinning, as shadowy faces peer down and the sound of muffled voices, echoing in the world of awakening dreams, brush past.

'Are you OK, Spud?' Monty asks, holding her hand so tight that she can feel her rings cut into her fingers.

'Where am I and how long have I been out?'

'You're home, safe, and you have been out nearly twelve hours,' replies Robyn.

'Twelve hours! I must have died. I've never passed out before.'

'Excuse me, the refrigerator in the morgue, remember,' says Sam, jokingly, but underneath relieved that her dearest friend is back with them.

'Oh. I forgot that one.'

'You forgot, now I'm beginning to worry,' laughs Sam, as Lizzy orders everyone out of the bedroom.

'You need to get some rest, my girl, that is an order, while I make you some hot soup.'

'I have already lost twelve hours,' she replies, leaping out of bed and grabbing her dressing gown. Lizzy growls, as she trips over herself trying to catch up, as Charity speeds her way to the kitchen and the others.

'You shouldn't be up, Spud,' says Monty, as he gently helps her to her seat.

'I'm fine, honey, really. Besides, I will go mad lying there just thinking.'

'You're not kidding. I mean, one minute I am human and the next I am a three-headed dolphin beast. What is going on? What did Polly mean by giving you back your name and look to your ancestors? I am scared, something's very wrong and I've a terrible feeling it all revolves around you.'

Charity looks at Robyn, her beautiful face etched with fear, the same look that she sees on everyone, but more so on Lizzy.

'Tell me what you know, Lizzy.'

Lizzy looks visibly shaken, trying to worm her way out of the one situation she prayed to avoid. 'I do not know what you mean, Charity, my darling. I'm just a silly old woman who keeps house and loves yah more than life itself.'

'No more lies, I have been kept in the dark long enough. All my life I have felt another presence inside me, a malevolent entity, like a malignant cancer that has been eating away at me, devouring my goodness.' The tears flow, she struggles to speak, her voice cracking, as her whole body trembles with sickness, the sickness of fear.

Lizzy's heart breaks. She cannot bear to see the pain on her beloved niece's face. She has protected her since birth, carrying the burden of the Merrick secret, hoping against hope that this day would never come.

'Do not cry, my darling, please do not cry. I cannot bear to see you hurting.'

'Then tell me the truth,' Charity yells, her whole body shaking with rage, as Lizzy recoils, frightened, not for herself, but for Charity.

Monty and the others sit up, shocked.

'It's all right, Spud. Everything is going to be OK.'

'No it won't, honey. I am afraid. For the first time in

my life, I do not feel in control. I have this powerful gift, and yet it is going to be my undoing, I know it.'

'Know what? What happened to you in Lucifer's underworld? How did you become this beast, which flew out from under his wings? What's going on?'

Deep down inside Monty feels afraid too. He has always felt it. Something sinister, unholy, that has been lurking in the shadows, waiting. Waiting to take his beloved Charity away from him and now it is closing in. Time's running out and the day of reckoning is coming. The day Lizzy has been dreading.

'I saw Annie.'

'Mum, you saw mum?' cries Robyn, excited, yet afraid, for what was her spirit doing in hell?

'There was a sorceress, Lucifer's queen of black witches, who came in the guise of Annie, who wasn't real, yet I know she was there. I heard her voice, calling to me, asking for help, she is in torment. Her soul incarcerated inside another. Lucifer has her.'

Robyn loses it, struggling to understand.

'But mum died of an illness, just like Ma, and is with the angels.' She turns, staring straight at Lizzy. 'How did mum really die?' she asks, angrily.

All eyes are upon Lizzy, her heart pounding faster and faster, as her body starts overheating, while her throat dries up. For once, she wishes she were not the centre of attention.

'We are waiting,' says Robyn, her voice cold and distant.

'A virus, my darling, she died of a virus,' she replies, her voice faint with the ring of panic.

'I do not believe you. You are lying. You say you love us, yet for all these years you have been lying to us,' shouts Robyn, as she turns on Charity.

'The famous Inceptor! Why did you not see through her lies? You can read the minds of spirits from another world, but you cannot read the mind of your own aunt.'

'Stop it. Stop it. I cannot bear it. Do not blame Charity. She is not the guilty one here. I am,' Lizzy cries, her heart racing, as her face turns purple and she collapses onto the floor.

'I am sorry, Lizzy, I am sorry. Forgive me. I did not mean those terrible things I said,' cries Robyn, helping Lizzy onto the chair and brushing the tears from her face. Charity wipes Lizzy's forehead with a cool, damp cloth, while the others look on, worried.

'It is all right, my darling. I knew this day would come. I just prayed it wouldn't,' she replies, suddenly looking her age as they see this feeble old woman gazing back at them. The strain of keeping the Merricks' dark secret finally tells on her, but more importantly, she hates not being able to share her burden with her loved ones. At least now she is free to tell what she knows as she slowly gathers her strength before beginning.

'Did you see Mary when you were taken by Lucifer?'

'No, but she came to me through the power of infallible thought, warning me against the Sorceress.'

Lizzy closes her eyes for a moment, catching her breath, before asking, 'Have you heard of the witch Hecate?'

'Yes, but legend has it that she was a goddess, whom the Romans worshipped.'

'That's right, my darling, but there is another legend written by the Roman scholar, Tacitus, who told of a Druid prophetess who evoked the goddess in one of her pagan rituals.'

'But the Druids were exclusively male, especially the high ranking ones,' says Robyn, interrupting.

'You are right, my darling, but the Celtic tribes who worshipped the Druidic ways often used Vates, or female witches, to evoke the magic of Wicca when practising divination. These Vates used sacrifices when performing their magic and it is said that a female sacrifice was used to summon the goddess Hecate.'

'Who was this goddess?' asks Jack, fascinated.

'She was a powerful Greek goddess, who was associated with magic and the underworld. Legend has it that she appeared in triple form, three women, back to back, representing the past, present and future. The Romans referred to her as the Mother Goddess, who came from the ancient world, where goddesses were an immensely powerful deity.'

'But these are just mythical stories; there are no such things as witches and goddesses,' laughs Leo, nervously.

'Just like shape-shifting beasts,' jokes Sam.

'We are losing track,' says Charity. 'What has this goddess and witch got to do with Ma and Annie?'

Lizzy shuffles her ample frame around in the chair, trying to get comfortable. 'I must go way back, my darling, to ancient mythical times, where spirits and demons wandered the earth and mortals worshipped them. So bear with me, my precious, as the story is long and dark, but needs to be told, if you are to understand who you are and where you come from.'

She draws a deep breath and begins.

'It began with the ancient Sumerians, who were a civilization that flourished around the fourth millennium BC, which today is known as modern Iraq. They believed the world was full of spirits who wandered between the two worlds. They worshipped the dark side of the spirit world, where they told of a ferocious evil spirit called Lilith. This spirit was a fierce, barren female demon who sported wings and talons on her feet and hands and who prowled the night skies searching for victims. She was reputed to be the first wife of Adam, whom God created as twins, joined together as one, but they fell out when

Adam insisted that, during sex, she lie beneath him. This angered her, as she felt they should be equal, and so, demanded her rights, which Adam refused. Lilith then left the heavenly gardens of Eden in a rage and made love to demons, giving birth to their children.

'God sent three angels, Sansanvi, Semangelaf and Sanvi after her. They caught up with her at the Red Sea, but she enjoyed her new-found freedom so much that she refused to return with them. This angered God. Therefore, he punished her by decreeing that every child conceived by her through demons would die in their tenth year. This so enraged her that she placed a maleficia (evil magic spell) on all newborn earthly children produced by her.

'So it began. She would fly through the night skies, accompanied by familiars in the form of owls and lions, shrieking her terrifying screams of the night beast, searching out sleeping men. She would then seduce them in their dreams in the form of beautiful angels, while her familiars sucked their blood. She spread her seed throughout the earth, until she gave birth to a hundred mortal babies, who survived God's decree, for the sperm was that of man, not demons. Yet they possessed the evil spirit of Lilith within them, and so she became immortal through her children, who begat more children and so on and so on, through time, until they became the deities known as the Druids, who have the power of the beast, also known as the shape-shifter within them.'

'What happened to Lilith?' asks Sam.

'When she had her one hundredth child, God took on the shape of the peregrine falcon, the fastest living creature on earth. He swooped down from the heavens, in the middle of the night, picked her up in his claws, and carried her into the fires of hell. But he needed to make sure that she could never spread her evil seed again, so flew through the seven gates of hell, which no spirit has ever survived, until he arrived at the depths of the underworld, where he left her.'

The room is so silent that you could hear the sound of a feather falling, as Leo asks, 'What are the seven gates and how come the peregrine survived the journey?'

'Each gate strips the spirit passing through it of its earthly comforts, clothing, desire, hope, love, possessions, power and finally its soul, until it arrives, naked, into hell. But our Lord, in the form of the peregrine falcon, was too fast to be caught within the gates, and so delivered Lilith to her fate.'

As Lizzy's dark tale unfolds, Monty's fear of losing Charity to the underworld returns, only this time it is more malevolent than ever.

Lizzy looks at her beloved niece and knows that she is beginning to understand.

'You are very quiet my darling?'

Charity looks at her, that look of awakening, when suddenly the secret pieces of her life begin to fit together.

'I read about the Druids in the *Book of Shadows*, which was shown to me many years ago by a white witch, who told me at the time that only those with the power of Wicca in them would understand its secrets. I told her that I was not a witch, but she said that one day I would know how to use its powers, that I was destined to use it, and that she had been waiting for me to come. The book felt strange, as if it wasn't real, just an illusion. I felt strangely drawn to it, but at the same time, afraid, so I left, not wanting to know more. And then I hear Annie ... for the first time since she died twelve years ago, when Robyn was only ten years old.'

Monty looks at her, as he realises something.

'What is it, honey, what's wrong?'

'You were ten years old when your mother died.'

Charity's heart stops. She had never made the connection before. Both their mothers died when they reached the age of ten, and both Robyn and she have the gift, whereas their mother's did not. Suddenly her mind goes into overdrive as she realises another startling 'coincidence'. Both Robyn's father and her own 'disappeared' when they were born. She discovered what happened to Pa, but Robyn's father is still a mystery. Annie never married. She always said that she got drunk one night at a party, had a one-night stand and Robyn was the result. She never talked of him again, and never attempted to find him.

Are these just coincidences? Robyn is afraid, something is very wrong. 'I do not think I want to know the secrets of the past, which I have a terrible feeling are about to call upon the present, to change the future, a dark future.'

All eyes are upon Lizzy, as Charity holds back, afraid to hear more. Jack tries to make sense of her tale so far.

'We have a Druid prophetess or Vate who summons a witch called Hecate, who comes in the form of three women. Then we have the Sumerians in the fourth millennium BC and the evil spirit, Lilith, who it seems spawned the Druid deity, which, as far as history tells, is extinct. Miss Charity escapes Lucifer's dark underworld in the form of a sea eagle spirit, and has suddenly acquired magical powers, turning us all into hybrid beasts. All the fathers disappear before the birth of their children and then the mothers die from a mysterious illness before their offspring reach their tenth year. Lizzy's dead sister is an angel, but Miss Charity's sister is a tortured soul in hell. We do not know who Robyn's father is, or if he is alive or dead. However, we do know that Miss Charity's father is now an angel. Stop me if I'm not making sense,' he says, catching his breath.

Leo and Sam look on, open-mouthed, as Charity smiles,

29

for this is the longest sentence she has ever heard Jack make, the no-nonsense one syllable tough man has found his voice.

'No, carry on, Jack, you are doing just fine,' says Charity.

He smiles that smug, male grin of his, which always appears when he is in control, and oh how he loves it.

'There must be a connection between Hecate and Lilith, which has to do with Miss Charity. One minute she is an inceptor with the power of the angels within her, and now, all of a sudden, she has the power to shape-shift into beasts and cast spells using the ancient art of witchcraft. And why does Lucifer relentlessly pursue her by sending false spirits to trap her?'

'When Annie was calling to me she said something about coming to me through the spirits of the Druid underworld, who had been waiting for me. Then she showed me the *Book of Shadows*, through my third-eye, and I was able to cast the spell of DAW, which just seemed to be within me. She said to call upon its magic and become who I am. Then Polly showed me the vision of a woman imprisoned in the underworld, existing only in the shadows, an empty shell. She has no soul. Why would Polly show me this woman? Who is she? And what is she to me?' Charity pauses. 'She said I had one more *final* quest to make, which would take me to the edge of the antediluvian world, where I would discover the truth of who I really am.'

Gently, she takes Lizzy's hand in hers, gripping it tightly, feeling that sickening lump of fear in her throat, as she struggles to ask the question, which Lucifer foretold, when he said, 'You cannot avoid your destiny. The beginning of the end has just begun.'

'Who am I, Lizzy...?'

30

6

The Vacuous Spirit

It is the longest of moments, when lifetimes go by in a second, and memories become dreams of the past, as Charity waits, praying that the darkness she has always felt within her is not real.

Monty can feel his strength ebbing away, terrified that his worst nightmare is becoming reality, while the RING wait in agonising anticipation.

'Know this, my darling. You are not evil. You must believe me. Your ancestors decreed your coming centuries ago. The darkness that haunts you is part of you; it is your other soul. It is you. Do not fight it, my darling, embrace it. To destroy your enemies you need to feel as they feel and think as they think, be as they are. Become them. To enter the jaws of darkness you must become it. You have the power of two within you: Hecate and Lilith.'

'No, no, this cannot be right. This is not happening,' she screams, her body faint with panic. 'Lilith was an evil spirit, who was glorified in the demonic underworld, and Hecate, according to your ancient tale, was a witch who required a female sacrifice by a Druid Vate before she could be summoned. I am not these evil creatures.'

Lizzy leaps off the chair, cradling her in her arms, as she weeps the tears of fear, while the others look on, stunned and helpless. Lizzy rocks Charity in her arms, while continuing the tale of Hecate and Lilith.

'The Druid prophetess, who summoned Hecate, had a vision in which she saw the coming of the King of Terror, who would bring with him the pestilence of death, which would spread like a plague throughout the earth, devouring everything that it touches, until all light, as we know it, is obliterated, and the new millennium of darkness begins.'

'But we destroyed him and all his children at the Battle of Kradlived, when Lucifer tried to evoke the power of darkness upon the earth. We won. Didn't we?' says Monty, his body shaking as the shiver of death runs through him.

'We won a battle, not the war, my darlings. You cannot destroy the Prince of Darkness. He comes in many forms and disguises. He is a malignant entity. An organic organism that absorbs all that it touches, growing stronger with each encounter, even in defeat, he wins. Each battle brings him closer to victory. He has been playing with us, drawing us in, draining our strength, and depleting our powers. He has waited, through the centuries of time, until this time.'

'I do not understand, what do you mean waiting for this time? What time?' asks Jack.

'I do not know when. I just know that it is in our time. It is in Charity's time, which is why Lucifer fears her so.'

Charity picks up, as she hears those words. 'What do you mean? Fears me? Why would he fear an enemy, who, according to you, can never destroy him?'

'He cannot be destroyed, but he can be stopped, and that is what he fears. You have the power of two within you, the power, which was reborn through witchcraft when Hecate was summoned.'

'How?'

'Once the prophetess had the vision she knew what

she must do. The Druids were dying and with them the Druidic ways. They are the only force that can stop the King of Terror and the one thousand years of darkness that he will bring, in the guise of man. So she summoned the goddess Hecate, who possessed the powers of the underworld, the witches' dark magic, which, if unleashed, could bring forth the beasts of both heaven and hell; the power of two.'

Lizzy's throat dries up, and she struggles to continue, as Sam brings her some water.

'Thank you,' she says, gulping it down.

'Now where was I? Oh, yes. She summoned Hecate with the promise of sacrificing herself.'

'So she didn't kill anybody?' asks Charity, her heart suddenly lifting.

'No, darling, she was a white Vate and practised only the ways of white magic. She knew, once she had the vision that her time had come, that she would have to call upon black magic. If you use black magic with pure intentions, then no harm will come to those who use it.

'Hecate, the powerful queen of the underworld came in the form of the triple goddess: Selene, the moon goddess; and Artemis, the goddess of nature, who between them had the power of the four elements: air, fire, water and earth. The prophetess told Hecate of her vision and asked for her help in return for her soul. Hecate accepted her sacrifice, but knew that black magic alone would not be enough to stop the coming of the thousand years of darkness, so evoked the spirit Lilith from the pit of hell, imprisoning her in the body of the prophetess. Hecate then bestowed the powers of the four elements of the triple goddess upon her, which, together with her shamanic powers of shape-shifting, made her the most powerful witch of all time. She possessed the powers of angels and demons, the light and dark side of the spirit world, and could summon spirits from both heaven and hell to do her bidding. She could transform herself into beasts from the spiritual and mortal world. She could live in both worlds, becoming whatever being she wanted to be, possessing whatever body she entered. She was all powerful.'

The RING sat motionless, soaking up every word of Lizzy's dark tale, until Robyn asked the question that Charity could not.

'What happened to the prophetess?'

'Hecate knew that she had created the most powerful being, whose powers should not be evoked until the King of Terror's prophesy becomes reality. Therefore, she imprisoned her shell of a body deep in the shadows of the underworld, but kept her soul within the heart of the triple goddess, protected by their powers, waiting for the female body of a Druid descendant, born with the powers of light and dark within her to unite them. Only then will the two become one.'

'But you said that if a witch uses black magic for good then no harm would come to her, yet she was condemned to the underworld with no soul,' says Robyn, watching Charity, who sits quietly waiting for Lizzy's answer.

'But you see, Robyn, my darling, no harm did come to her. She did not die. She feels no pain or sadness. She exists only in the shadows. She has no concept of time. She sleeps the sleep of the vacuous spirit, waiting to be awakened.'

All eyes turn to Charity.

'Am I that descendant?'

Lizzy cradles her so tight that she almost crushes the life from her.

'That you are, my darling.'

'Why was I never told of this before? Why keep me in the dark? Moreover, why has my Lord never shown me the vision of my past?

'To carry the knowledge of who you are through life would have been too much of a burden to bear. It is only now that Lucifer has shown himself at the Court of Past Souls, where Ma and Annie contacted you, evoking your powers through the *Book of Shadows*, that we know it is time, your time...'

7

The Agreement

The night draws in and the strain of the day overcomes
them, as Charity's strength fails her. Usually the thrill of
a new quest would stimulate her whole being, but this
time the charge is she. Instead of pushing her body
beyond its limits into the early hours seeking clues to
dark secrets and unanswered questions, she wishes only
sleep. To sleep through a lifetime, waking only when this
nightmare has dissipated, and her life returned to before.
But although her body is shattered, her mind is exploding,
fearful of what souls from the spirit world will visit her
tonight through the doorway into her dreams. She is
tired, so very tired, but afraid to close her eyes, as this
time she knows the messages within her dreams will
become reality when she wakes.

So many questions race through her mind. Who is this
King of Terror? Is he man or beast, spirit or demon?
When and where will he come and how will she know
who he is? How will she find him and how will she stop
him? What is the one thousand years of darkness? How
and when is it to happen? Where is the edge of the
antediluvian world? Moreover, what is its significance?
How will she find the *Book of Shadows*, which the witch
foretold she was destined to use? Why did Annie and
Ma die when she and Robyn reached the age of ten

36

years? What really happened to Robyn's father and does she really know the truth about her own? Moreover, what of Ma and Annie, where do they fit into this labyrinth of unholy secrets? Why is Annie a tortured soul when Ma is an angel? Why was she chosen to become the descendant of the Druid prophet? Who is she really, witch or angel, demon or divine spirit? How will she and the vacuous spirit join the power of two, to become one? What is the power of two? How will she use it and what will become of her and the RING when she does? Who and where are these Druid ancestors, which, according to Annie, are waiting for the coming? What is the coming? Is it she or the Antichrist? Or the end of the world as we know it?

The questions keep on coming, but the answers are empty. Lizzy was right. To be afflicted with the enormity of this time from birth would have been the cruellest and darkest of burdens to endure. Today Charity's innocence has gone forever and her journey into the fissure of the underworld has just begun.

She closes her eyes, wishing for the longest and deepest of sleeps, as she feels the warmth of Monty's body beside her. If only she could trap this moment in time, as he places his muscular arms around her, cocooning her in his strength.

'Wake up, Charity, wake up.'

The voice grows louder and louder until she finds herself sitting up in bed, looking around, to see Monty fast asleep beside her. It's four o'clock in the morning and the room is still dark, with just a glimmer of the early morning sky filtering through the split in the curtains, forming a beam of light in the centre of the room, which moves upwards until there is a channel of energy reaching from the earth into the world of spirits. Charity rubs her eyes and then it appears. A phantom spirit...

37

The light transforms into a magical waterfall running into a river of pure light, dazzling in its splendour. She walks out of the waterfall, naked, part woman, part jaguar, with droplets of water dripping from her into the river, forming sparkling fairies, which buzz and fly around her, as they drink the waters of eternal life. A vision of womanhood, with beautiful pale, shimmering skin, perfect long legs and arms, a creature desired by men and emulated by women. Her face majestic, her smile mesmerising, as she moves towards Charity, arms out-stretched, willing her to embrace them. However, as she draws closer Charity sees pointed ears growing from her forehead. Her hair is rough and tufted upon her head as it trails down her back ending in a thin line at the tip of her tail, her body a sea of spots; the jaguar cat. She is the embodiment of the shape-shifter, who breathes life into all that she touches, empowering all. She comes only when summoned by the gods.

'Do not be afraid, Charity. I bring you the gift of the four elements sent to you by Hecate. Bathe in the waters of eternal life. Be reborn and claim your birthright, the demons' magic, passed down to you by your true mother, Lilith. Let the dark side into your soul and Hecate, your protector, will show you the way. Come, Charity, let me baptise you in the lake of eternal life.'

Charity leaps at her, screaming. 'I have a mother and she is with my Lord and I was conceived through the love of mortals, not a witch. Lilith is not my mother. My mother guides and protects me from the heavens. She will come. I know she will. You are false, sent by the Antichrist to trick me.'

The jaguar-woman prowls around her, purring and licking her face with her rough tongue, while curling her tail around her body, catlike. 'She will not come. She cannot. She is *nullipara* and can only watch from the heavens, where your Lord has sent me to you through the power of Hecate. Trust in your gift and feel the blood of Lilith racing through your veins and embrace the powers that are yours by right of birth.'

Charity's blood is raging, as she grabs her by the scruff of the neck, hurling her through the air and back into the waterfall.

'*Nullipara* – that means a woman who has never given birth. My mother conceived me. I have seen pictures of her when she was with child. You lie. This dream is a lie. Everything is a lie and soon I will awake from this nightmare and all will be as it was.'

The spirit laughs as she shakes the water from her, swiftly moving her feline body through the air until they are face to face, their eyes fixed as they stare each other down, neither giving the other the scent of defeat. The jaguar sniffs her prey, but Charity does not flinch.

'I smell your anger, but feel your strength. You are fearless, Charity. You are your mother's daughter.'

'I possess the power of the angels bestowed upon me by the one true God. I am the Inceptor, whose gift is that of the heavens and not the underworld. I am not the daughter of an evil spirit reincarnated as a Druid witch. I am not this evil creature. I am not she,' she screams, holding back the tears for fear of showing weakness to her adversary, who stops laughing.

'What you see is not always what is and to know one thing of a person does not mean that you know them.'

She steps back, her feline body gracefully returning to the waterfall, as the fairies flicker around her and the light of the heavens glows upon her. She raises her right hand and the waters part. 'Look back into the past, Charity, look and see.'

Charity sees her parents in a doctor's surgery. They are young and in love, as they sit holding hands tightly, waiting for the news that will alter the destinies of their lives forever. The doctor calls them in, but he is sombre, as they listen to his diagnosis.

'I am sorry to tell you that you will never be able to have children, Mrs Merrick. It is an inherited disease, to which I am afraid there is no medical cure. I am very sorry to be the bearer of such sad news.' His voice carries over them as he continues to talk. They are numb with disbelief and grief as all their dreams of becoming proud parents dissipate into an empty, barren future.

'But that is all we want, to have a child, to love and nourish it, protect and guide it into adulthood. It has to be a mistake. I feel perfectly healthy. What is this inherited disease and why has my family never told me about it? No, you are wrong. Your receptionist has mixed up your patients' notes; these things happen all the time, you have to check your records again, please. It is a terrible mistake. I cannot have our dreams stolen from us like this. You must be able to do something. Help us, doctor, please, you must help us,' she pleads as the doctor sits quietly, listening, while she falls apart in front of him. He slowly says, in that sympathetic but creepily detached manner of his:

'I am afraid there is no mistake, Mrs Merrick, but I want to help. I can see your devastation and feel your anguish. There is a way that you can conceive a child of your own, if you are both willing?'

'Anything, doctor, we are willing to do anything,' she replies. Her body and voice are animated with renewed hope as she wipes the tears from her face, while her husband, although shocked, tries to remain calm.

'Just a minute, darling, we need to discuss this first

before committing to anything, which I am sure, doctor, you would agree.'

'Of course, of course, you have both had a terrible shock and need time to come to terms with everything, but, unfortunately, if I am to help you, I am afraid time is something we do not have,' he replies compassionately, but underneath there hides a far more sinister being.

'I thought you wanted the same as me, our own child, and now the doctor is offering this precious gift and you want to think about it,' she cries, desperately clinging onto his hand as he looks into her tortured face, crying inside for his love, afraid that if he does not agree with the doctor's proposal he will lose not only a child, but his wife as well. Against his better judgement, he finds himself agreeing to listen to the doctor's offer of help.

'I have a private clinic where I help unfortunate couples like you, who are unable to have children of their own. In your case, Mrs Merrick, you do not have the ability to ovulate or produce eggs of your own, so we would have to use the eggs of another woman, a donor. Sadly, a patient of mine, whose eggs we have frozen, has just died along with her husband in a car crash, and her parents have requested that I destroy her eggs. If I help you, I will be breaking the law, but I feel it would be sacrilege to destroy them when they could give you both the precious gift of a new life. The parents have requested that they be present at the destruction of the eggs, which will be at four o'clock tomorrow.

'Therefore, you see my dilemma, Mr and Mrs Merrick. I am in a position to offer you both your dream of a child, but at a price, that price being that the child's genes will be that of another woman, whose family must never know of what we have done. And I'm afraid you must make your decision now so that I can operate on you both, tonight.'

41

'Why both of us, surely you just need to operate on my wife?'

'The particular disease your wife has means that she cannot keep the eggs in her womb long enough for your sperm to impregnate them. Therefore I would need to take your sperm and the eggs, impregnating your wife immediately, and then keep her in hospital for observation until I am satisfied that the pregnancy will go the full term.'

'I don't know. It is all very quick and I need to think. I want a child, but it will not be ours, and what of the moral issues here? We must respect the wishes of this tragic couple's family. Why would you be willing to put your career in jeopardy by breaking the Hippocratic oath for a couple you hardly know, doctor? What is really in it for you? What do you really want from us? Because if it is money, we do not have it,' he says, suspecting that this doctor is not all that he seems, but she can only see the child, a beautiful baby of her own, which would be hers, as she carries it in her womb, feeding and nourishing it, feeling it grow inside her. Her dream would finally become reality, a temptation that she is unable to resist, no matter the consequences.

'My husband didn't mean it, doctor. We are grateful for what you are doing for us and I want this child, more than life itself. Please, doctor, whatever it takes, we will do it,' she says, looking at her husband, desperate for his agreement. He knows he has already lost, and that there will be a heavy price to pay in the future for the sin they are about to commit.

'Excellent, we have an agreement, which, for obvious reasons, must not be of the written word, but from one soul to another,' replies the doctor, smiling, as they shake hands and the agreement is sealed.

'But what about the family's wishes, that they watch you destroy the eggs?'

42

'Do not worry yourself, Mrs Merrick, I will take care of everything, you just concentrate on your beautiful new baby, which will soon be yours.'

The vision disappears, as Charity screams, 'No, wait, please wait, what happened to Ma and Pa and who am I?'

The jaguar glides closer, wrapping her feline body around her, purring seductively as she whispers, 'You are the last descendant of the children of Lilith. Your earthly mother was the vessel, used to conceive the last child of the hundredth child, you. Your birth was decreed when the triple goddess Hecate foresaw the coming of the King of Terror. You are the only one that can stop him, Charity. You are the one.'

'No, you are wrong, my niece, Robyn, she is a descendant. I am not the last and her mother died, like mine, when she was ten years old.'

'You are the last, Charity. Lilith reversed God's decree when she placed a maleficia on her earthly born children. When they reached their tenth year, their mothers would die and their souls would be condemned to hell to join her demon children, sent there by God in their tenth year.'

'But Ma's soul is in heaven!'

'God saved her, for he knew that she would protect you until this time. She has always been there, watching over you, protecting you and yours.'

'But what of Annie, why was she not saved and why is Robyn not the last descendant?'

'Because.'

'Because what?' yells Charity, angrily.

'Annie is not your sister...'

'Not my sister,' she shouts, holding her head in her

43

hands, while yet another knife strikes through her heart. 'No, no, I cannot bear this any more. First, you tell me my mother is not my real mother, now my sister is not my sister. Is there nothing in my life that is real? Who is Robyn's mother?'

'I cannot tell you. Only her mother can, when she is ready.'

'But Robyn, poor Robyn, what of her, what am I to tell her?'

'Nothing, tell her nothing. Her time will come soon enough. Let her enjoy her innocence a bit longer.'

'But the gift, she has it too. Where does it come from if my sister is not my sister?'

'No more questions. I have come by divine decree to show you the vision of your past, so that the present can take you into the future. I can tell you only this ... you have three mothers. Lilith, whose spirit gives you the dark power of the witch's black magic. Hecate, the triple goddess and your protector from the underworld, who will show you the power of the four elements. And finally, Mary, your earth mother, who gave you your human form, which together with your shamanic powers of the shape-shifter makes you the most powerful being on earth.'

Suddenly she stops, as they become still and Charity sniffs the air like an animal.

'What is it? What's wrong?' Charity asks, as the two of them stand back to back, stalking the room, two magnificent creatures protecting their territory. The animal within them smells the blood of another, a predator, sent to destroy them.

Instinctively Charity feels different, as if she is two people, one inside who is still she and the other, who has stepped out of her body and is watching herself, yet she is still the same person. As they circle the room, she no longer feels angry and confused. Instead she feels strangely content, as if she has awoken from a deep sleep and everything is slowly making sense. She suddenly feels at one with her new powers and is no longer afraid, indeed, she feels invincible. How can she suddenly accept who she is and that Ma was not her natural mother? Moreover, why does she no longer fear her other mothers, Lilith and Hecate?

'What is happening to me?' she whispers under her breath; she curls her body around her feline friend, as they continue to stalk the room.

'The power of two is becoming one within you, Charity. Soon you will be united with your other soul, and then you will know all. First, we must destroy the beast that hides in the shadows, waiting to strike. You must make it to the lake otherwise all is lost.'

They stop, dead centre, as they smell it. The jaguar prepares for the kill, her teeth bared and her body crouched, ready to pounce, as Charity's shamanic powers transform her into a black leopard, part woman, part leopard, her body pure animal, sleek and black, with sharp claws, ready to strike. Her head is that of a leopard, with its catlike ears growing from her forehead, antennaes that listen to every sound that whispers in the air. She has a long mane of blond hair running down her back, magnificent against her black cat body; her face is split into two, one side human, and one side leopard. The cat and the woman, two powers in one, the instincts of the animal and the intelligence of the mortal, both seeking out the enemy.

Then they see it...

First, the eyes; flaming red eyes like the fires of hell, as it emerges from the shadows, the devil-man, part man, part demon. He floats towards them, his body human and rippling with muscles, naked in all its glory, his powerful legs fused together forming a tail, which can cut its prey in two. His face is handsome in a dark, demonic way, which mesmerizes all that look upon it, yet once close up death is your only companion. Growing from his head are antlers, symbolising his sexual powers over all, both man and woman, for he is the devil-demon and all souls are his for the taking. In his left hand he wields the burning sword of Lucifer, his creator and master, which, with one stroke, will set you aflame, sending you into hell, burning in agony for all eternity. The only reprieve from the fire of eternal death is when Lucifer commands your soul to do his bidding, in demon form. He has many burning souls pleading for release from their eternal torture. The devil-man never loses a soul, which is why Lucifer chose him and why he is confident that she will soon be his...

He smiles, that dazzling, hypnotic smile, which, as he slithers closer, seduces them with his virile body until, finally, they succumb. They drop their guard, and he is almost upon them, raising his left hand and thrusting his flaming sword in the air.

Down he strikes, the flames so hot that they can smell their flesh burning, which awakens the animal. They leap, snarling and scratching into the air, sinking their teeth into his arm, tearing into his flesh, drawing blood as he recoils in agony, swinging his arm back and forth, while they grip tighter and tighter until they crunch into his bones. He screams in agonising pain, as they cling onto his arm with their powerful jaws, sinking their claws into his body, ripping the flesh from his muscles, as he swings back and forth, trying desperately to release himself from their deadly grip. They hiss and spit, as he spins them around the room, their bodies flying in the air with his, but still he cannot release himself. His blood flows down onto the floor into a river of red. He swings his mighty tail up into the air, then down, striking them with its

46

powerful blow, sending them spiralling through the air, landing on the other side of the room, away from the lake.

His body is bloody and ripped to shreds, but not beaten, as he wields his flaming sword, lashing his tail back and forth, raising his antlers in the air, defiantly, baiting them.

Three predators divided by a river of blood, stalking their territory, each waiting to see who will strike first. The jaguar and leopard, prowling up and down, contemplating their next move, while the devil-man waits, knowing that they must get to the lake.

The cats divide, leaping at him from both sides, knowing that he will not be able to stop the two of them, but he does not move, as they fly at him with bared teeth and claws. He sways his mighty antlers, cutting through them both as they tumble to the ground, wounded and bleeding into the river of blood. Triumphantly, he floats over them, running his tail over their bodies, as they lie dazed and beaten, unable to fight back.

'I am sorry I failed you, Charity, forgive me,' cries the jaguar, as the devil-man thrusts his sword into her, exploding her body into flames, while the fires of hell rise up from the underworld, carrying her screaming into hell.

'I thought you would be harder to kill, Charity,' he says laughing, while bending down to gloat.

She looks up, staring into his demon eyes, whispering, 'You were right...'

He stops laughing. She is upon him, her jaws locked around this throat, sinking into his neck, ripping it clean out, as he crumbles to the ground, floating in his own river of blood. She rises up, victorious, looking down to see his flaming sword lying beside him.

'I am sure there are many souls eager to greet you with a very, very warm welcome,' she says, coldly, picking

47

up his sword and swinging it in the air before plunging it down, striking through the heart, as he feels the fire of hell erupting inside him and hears the last piercing cry of death. His master will not be merciful...

Charity is still, as she looks around her bedroom and sees Monty asleep, oblivious to the dark battles that come to her in the night through the doorway of her dreams. She looks at the waterfall and lake, two worlds existing in a dream that is not a dream. How surreal it all feels, yet to her it is normal. For as long as she can remember she has lived on the edge of these two worlds, each crossing over into the other, pulling at her, eating away at her soul, until she can no longer distinguish between the two. She has become a vessel, half-filled, part mortal, part spirit, but neither complete. She grips the red disk around her neck, rubbing it slowly, reminding herself that both worlds are real. The globe of the world, protecting the angel of true sight that hangs from a chain of human spirits, which one day she may have to summon. This is her proof that the dream is real. That she is real. That one day, soon, the doorway will close and the vessel will be full ... but which half will it be?

Suddenly she feels herself flying, as her body is carried by the lake fairies to the waterfall, where they suspend her, as it tumbles down over her, invigorating her with its icy cold touch. It feels wonderful, as she closes her eyes and wallows in its purity. Never before has she felt such calmness, such clarity, such gentleness, such all encompassing power and strength; she feels insuperable. The water enters every orifice, filling her up, until she becomes impregnable, as her skin glows and her eyes burn with the light of eternal life.

She is reborn as the waters baptise her.

While the water flows, she can feel herself changing. All her doubts and fears wash away into the lake as she

48

becomes revitalised and a new Charity Holmes emerges. The fairies carry her back to her bed, where they tenderly lay her down, whispering, 'Sleep Charity, sleep deep, for tomorrow your final quest begins...'

8

Coincidences

'Good morning, Spud, and how is my beautiful psychic today?' asks Monty, as he turns over, kissing her gently on the cheek, while she stretches out, slowly opening her eyes.

'Hmm, the room feels different, yet I cannot put my finger on it,' he says, looking around, sensing that something has happened, but what? The bedroom looks the same, yet it is not. 'You have had one of your dreams, haven't you?'

'I cannot slip anything past you, my love,' she replies, grinning.

'What is that smirk I see? Something's happened and I suspect by that big grin on your face that it was pretty significant.'

'Let's just say that I have come to terms with my past and the future will be determined by my present.'

'Here we go again. When you start the day talking in riddles then I know my Spud is back and that all hell, figuratively speaking, is just about to break loose,' he says, holding her tightly, happy to see the sparkle back in her eyes, a sparkle that somehow shines brighter than ever before, which, for a moment sends a cold chill right through him, but he shrugs it off. He has his Charity back and that is all that matters for now.

'You know you could always wake me up when you are having one of your dreams; after all, I do not see why you should have all the fun,' he says, as they enter the kitchen.

'You would only find them boring, my love, besides, you need your beauty sleep more than me,' she jokes.

Everyone, especially Lizzy, is secretly relieved to hear laughter in her voice again. For just a few hours ago, all they could see was her crumbling before them, destroyed by so many secrets. What would the RING do without her? She *is* the RING, the centre of their world, the one who shows them the way and keeps them strong. Without her certainty and belief in who she is they are lost. The RING and inceptor are two halves of the same circle; break it and it loses its power, but complete it becomes impenetrable.

There is an unspoken uneasiness in the air, while Lizzy serves breakfast. The love between them is stronger than ever, but where there was certainty there is now doubt, and where there was trust there is now wariness, not of each other, but of what is out there. Yesterday their world changed forever. They can no longer trust anyone or anything. All they have is each other, the RING against the underworld, a dark evil world that is coming for theirs, only this time, they are not sure if they can win...

Charity watches Lizzy and Robyn from the corner of her eye, the niece whose mother is not her sister. Does this mean she is not her aunt? But Robyn is still Robyn and she could not love her any more no matter what her parentage. Then there is Lizzy, who held her in her arms when she was a child and who has been her rock all through her life. She watches her closely. Trying to see inside her, but her gift is useless when the sight is blind. Love is blind and Charity cannot get past that. She knows that Lizzy is hiding more secrets, but senses that this is not the time for revelations. She can wait and trusts in her aunt to do the right thing at the right time. How comforting it is to have this inner peace, which she never felt before. She was always fighting some dark inner self, her other half, which until her dream last night, she feared, but no more. Even though she still does not feel complete or know all the answers to all the questions, she knows one thing: that the end is coming...

'What is ticking away in that brain of yours, Spud? How about sharing those thoughts?' asks Monty, watching her protectively.

'Sorry, honey,' she replies, pulling herself back from the world of thoughts into reality. 'Just trying to make sense of it all so far.'

'Well from what Lizzy said yesterday your destiny has already been mapped out, and you, or we, have no choice but to follow it,' says Robyn, sensing that Charity is different, that she is holding something back, connected to her, but sees that it is out of love and not deceit, and so says nothing. Everyone is protecting everyone else, all waiting for each other to break the silence of untold secrets, which seem to multiply by the hour.

Charity looks at her family, who sit there, nervously pretending that everything is OK, but underneath they know it is not. They all feel it, that inexplicable knowing that their world is about to change forever. You can almost taste the trepidation in the air, the feeling that there may not be too many more cosy meals like this together, that the RING is facing its last quest, which will seal their fate forever...

'What is your decision, my darling?' asks Lizzy, shaking, fearful at her reply.

'Like Robyn said, we have no choice, we must go on until the end, no matter what the outcome. If we do not the end will come, but will not be of our choosing,

but of another, whose world is not a place of enlighten-
ment.'

'I agree. This is a war, and if we do not fight, extinction
of our world, as we know it, will be the result,' says Jack,
always the soldier.

'We have always done everything together,' says Sam,
rubbing her ring, while looking around at her family, her
adopted family, and the only real thing in her life. She
reads the inscription inside: 'If this is to be our last quest
together, then let it be the best.' Her eyes well up and
her voice cracks. They all sit silently, soaking up the
strength from each other. Charity watches, as the purple
aura of courage circles them, encasing them in its mystical
light.

She closes her eyes, capturing the moment, freezing it
in her mind's eye, and holding onto it for as long as
possible, knowing that nothing or no one can ever take
this precious gift of total oneness from her. Whatever
happens in the future, the present will always be there,
stored in her mind's eye, which will comfort her when
the dark days come.

'There are no coincidences, just fragments of life that
happen in no order or time, but when pieced together
they form the pictures of our lives.'

'What do you mean, Spud?'

'There are three kinds of people in the world, the ones
who see, the ones who do not and the ones who turn
away.'

'I do not understand? What are you saying, Spud?'

'I see that the RING was meant to be, that it was no
coincidence that we all met in our own separate ways to
become one. I was born with a purpose, decided long
before I breathed my first breath of life. You were born
with a purpose, decided by the gods, long before your
mother conceived you and we met. Everyone's destiny is

decided before life begins, but it is only those who see that can truly understand and know their fate.'

'Are you saying that you see our fate? Why didn't you tell us before and why didn't we see it ourselves?' asks Leo.

'Although I have the gift I could never see my own sign, until yesterday. I believe you can too.'

'Believe what?' asks Monty.

'In yourself, honey, in yourself.'

'But what about those who do not see and those who turn away, what happens to them?' asks Sam.

'Life is like a jigsaw puzzle. Some people can look and eventually see where the missing pieces should be, and so begins the real journey of their life, a second chance to live again, the right way. Others, no matter how hard they look, cannot see and so never complete the puzzle, leaving them to travel a path that never feels fulfilled. The third kind see the missing pieces, but cannot or will not complete the puzzle, and so turn away. These are the most wretched of people, who saw and did nothing, but always carry the picture of what they might have been within them, tortured souls who lost their second chance.'

Nobody moves, listening to the silence, the silence of destiny calling.

'So what happened yesterday, my darling, to make you see?' asks Lizzy.

'I had a dream, where some of the pieces of the jigsaw of my life came together and I saw who I was meant to be. For the first time I see my true path, which is intrinsically linked to all of you, my beloved family, but the puzzle is not complete and so we must search for the final pieces of the true journey of our lives.'

'Phew, I guess this means that cosy nights in with the wife watching TV are out for the time being?' jokes Leo, as he squeezes Sam's hand tightly.

'You would only be complaining about getting fat anyway, my love,' she replies, laughing, yet secretly terrified, trying desperately to be brave, when all she really wants to do is go to bed and pull the bed covers over her, hiding like a small child until the bogeyman has gone.

'So where do we begin this journey of ours?' asks Monty.

'Home.'

'But we are home!'

'The other home, honey, we must go to Holmes House...'

'Now I am confused. What has Holmes House to do with this?' asks Monty, feeling distinctly uncomfortable.

'I do not know. I just feel we must go there. I cannot explain why except to say that once we are there we will see the sign.'

'What sign?' asks Jack.

'I cannot see it yet. I just know our journey begins there, where Monty and I were married and our paths became the same.'

Monty looks at her, suddenly realising what she meant by 'there are no coincidences'. As soon as they met, he knew that she was the one, his other soul, and the missing piece of himself, the final piece of the jigsaw.

'We pack and leave today. Robyn, cancel all my appointments. If anyone asks why, say that I am going away on an extended vacation, but do not tell them where. Lizzy, do the usual when we close up the house for winter, informing everyone that we are going on one of our expeditions abroad and will not be contactable for some time, as we are not sure where we will be or when we will be back. Sam and Leo, I need you both to come with us, but you cannot tell anyone where you are going or for how long.'

'Why the secrecy and why not tell our friends?' asks Leo.

55

'Because there are no coincidences...'

Leo and Sam look at each other, as it slowly dawns on them what she means. All their friends, their work colleagues, associates, their life, which they thought they had carefully created by their own choices and decisions suddenly become just pieces of a puzzle, a puzzle that they assumed they had made, but now they see that it was already there, slowly being put together by other forces.

Jack says nothing, as he looks at Monty and Charity. Wherever they go, he goes. She does not need to ask. He is their constant companion and protector. From the moment his path crossed with Monty's, they knew that they would be friends until death. A friendship like theirs is the rarest of things, where two people meet from different worlds; Monty, the aristocrat, and Jack, the rough diamond, but both equal in their respect for each other. They are more than friends; they are the brothers they never had. Then Charity comes along and his family is complete, the only family he has ever known. There was nothing and no one before them and there will be nothing after them; his life began with them.

There are no coincidences...

9

The Black Mirror

They arrive in the dead of night, as Jack opens the
electric iron gates and begins the drive up the long
shingled path that leads to Holmes House, while Sam
and Leo follow in their car. As soon as Charity sets eyes
upon this imposing house, she feels a chill. She has never
liked it. It has always been Monty's home, never hers.
His parents never liked her; the 'common tart', was his
mother's favourite words for her. She was the 'whore'
that robbed them of an heir. She has never been able to
bear Monty a child, although there are no medical reasons
to explain why. She was never good enough for their son
and they were relentless in their quest to destroy their
marriage, but Monty loves her with a passion. Even now,
after all these years, she still cannot believe how enduring
and passionate their love is. They come from such different
worlds, but when together, they are as one soul.

The house is Monty's now, bequeathed to him when
his parents died. First to go was his father, leaving his
mother desolate and inconsolable, for although she was
a cold and distant woman, she was nothing without her
partner. He was the love of her life and the reason for
her existence. When he died of a heart attack she died
of a broken heart two years later. Charity still feels their
presence. It is their house and always will be and so she

comes here only when she must, preferring to stay in London, her real home, which Monty and she bought together and where her hallway spirits watch over her. The spirits in Holmes House are cold and unfriendly. They hark back to a time and place when the likes of Charity Merrick were beaten and kept in their place. They do not welcome her into their home, and when they visit her during the dead of night, they come to taunt and mock, sent by Monty's cowardly parents, who dare not show themselves for fear of her gift. If only they could be happy for their son and accept what is, they would not languish in the 'middle life' as tortured spirits, but rejoice in the afterlife, which awaits them once they let go of their bitterness.

She never tells Monty of these nasty spirits that creep around his house, torturing her with their whispers. He must never know of the darkness that lurks in his parents' souls; it would destroy him. And so she tolerates them, but if they ever hurt him, it would be their undoing, and so they show themselves only to her.

They settle in for the night and already Charity can feel the hairs rise at the back of her neck, as she hears their screeches and sees their grey shapeless forms seeping through the walls, coming to taunt her through the long dark night, which seems endless, as Monty sleeps peacefully beside her.

The kitchen is buzzing, as Lizzy takes charge, infuriating Kathy and Jim Moggs, the live-in housekeeper and grounds man, who have been looking after Holmes House for the past 20 years. She is small and scrawny with dark, lank hair tied back in a thin ponytail and speaks in an irritating high-pitched voice. He is tall and wiry with watering eyes and bad teeth and always does what his wife says. He is the brawn and she the brains. They cannot stand Lizzy, who bosses them around and takes over everything whenever she visits. She upsets their comfortable world where they have the run of the house and staff to themselves, with only Monty and Jack to look after on their occasional visits and the odd function such as the annual summer ball and Christmas gathering. Lizzy feels they act above their station, and so takes great pleasure in putting them in their place, which Monty secretly enjoys watching. They do fancy themselves as Lord and Lady of the house, and so it tickles him to see them squirm a little, even though he wouldn't be without them, as they look after him like a son, which he takes comfort in. They are constantly complaining about Lizzy, but he just smiles, telling them that it is just her way and that they should not get so upset. Therefore they scowl around the house, bossing the other staff around even more, who cringe whenever they see Lizzy arriving, because they know that they are in for a hard time from Lord and Lady 'Muck'.

'Now that we are all here what do we do next? Where is this sign that you are seeking and when do you think we will be returning to London? After all, I am a judge and have trials coming up and people will be chasing me. I cannot even answer my mobile for fear of something, but what?'

Charity looks at Leo, who suddenly seems very fragile. He has lost the commanding persona of the judge presiding over his court; instead she sees a bewildered and frightened middle-aged man trying to hold onto his dignity and pride. What does she say to him and the others? That her new powers are telling her that she will never be going back to London, yet will not show her why? That she just had to come to Holmes House where Polly's words echo throughout; words that told her that she must go back to the beginning, where the end is the beginning. This is not where she was born or raised, so why does she feel so drawn to it?

She looks at Monty, who is tucking into a hearty breakfast before going on his early morning ride over the rolling Somerset hills on his favourite black stallion, Fagan, a present from her on their first wedding anniversary. There are happy memories here: their wedding at the nearby village of Grimoire, where her new life began and those dark days of feeling 'different' from everyone else disappeared, as she became Charity Holmes.

She sees it now. This is where she was born again, where she reinvented herself and left her old life behind. It has to be here, and it begins at the ancient church of Grimoire, where they were married.

'Do not worry, Leo, I have a feeling that you will be sorting things out fairly soon, so just relax and enjoy the fresh air and beautiful countryside. As for the sign, I believe we will find it at the church of Grimoire.'

Monty stops eating and looks at her, startled. Their wedding was the happiest day of his life. Before she came into his life, he always felt a longing, a sadness, an emptiness inside him. Yes, he had a privileged life and many beautiful women who he could have married, but she was the one. She was not the intellectual equal or the most beautiful of the women he was used to dating, but she captivated him. He could see right into her soul, which touched his, filling him up until he was empty no more. He would be devastated if the church where they pledged their unity together turned out to be another one of Lucifer's hidden underworlds, concealed in a cloak of respectability; their sacred vows, tainted forever, by his presence.

'Why there?' he asks, angry, but also afraid. Afraid of what they will uncover.

60

She feels his pain and so is careful to say only what is required. 'I need to find the *Book of Shadows*, which will protect and guide us in our quest. I feel the book is hidden there, which the witch foretold I was destined to use.'

'But what makes you think the book is hidden in the church?'

'The name Grimoire, I know what it means.'

'Grimoire?' he asks.

'It means book containing magical spells that is passed down through the centuries to those who hold the power of Wicca. The *Book of Shadows*; it is there, waiting for me.' She stops. 'There are no coincidences...'

Everyone loses their appetites, as they suddenly feel sick. That stomach churning sickness when your whole life seems out of control, where you sense that an unseen force is manipulating it, which, at any given moment, can decide your fate.

'Jim, you had better tell the stable lad to unsaddle Fagan, as it looks like we are going into the village this morning,' yells Monty.

'No, go on your ride, honey, I know how much you love it,' she says, wanting him to feel the power of Fagan underneath him, as the two of them ride like the wind on the wild Somerset hills. Riding Fagan is his only other passion. It lifts his spirit beyond this world into a place where he is totally free, where nothing or no one can touch him; Fagan and him, wild spirits that roam the hills, fearless and free. She will not take that from him.

'But I am coming with you, Spud. You are not to go there without me,' he says, worried that she will cut him out, trying to protect him, but he will not have it. They are in this together, all the way to the end, whatever that might be...

'It's OK, honey. I have things to do here first, so we

61

will go after lunch. The book has waited for centuries; it can wait a few more hours.'

Monty looks at her. 'You will not sneak off without me?'

'No, honey, I promise. We will go to Grimoire after lunch.'

'Jim,' he yells. 'Cancel that last instruction, I will be riding Fagan.'

'I wish he would make his bloody mind up, who does he think we are, his servants?' he moans, walking back to the stable yard, yelling at the stable lad: 'Saddle him up again, Mr Holmes is riding after all.'

'What. I have just un-tacked him.'

'Do not answer back, you moron, just do what I say.'

'Do this, do that, fucking Lord Muck,' he groans under his breath.

'What did you say?'

'Nothing, Mr Moggs.'

'You had better watch your attitude my lad otherwise you will find yourself out on your ear.'

'Yes, sir,' he replies, scowling, while Fagan stomps around neighing excitedly, eager for his master to arrive so that they can fly with the wind together; masters of all they oversee.

'Kathy, I need the keys to the house, all of them.'

'Why, Mrs Holmes, I can open any locked doors for you?' she replies, reluctant to hand over control of Holmes House.

'I know, Kathy, but I do not know exactly which rooms I want to look in and how long I will be, and so do not wish to keep you hanging on when I am sure you have better things to do.'

'But I do not mind, Mrs Holmes,' she says anxiously, hating the thought of Charity poking around in her house.

'I absolutely insist, Kathy, now the keys please.'

'Very well, Mrs Holmes, but I still do not understand why you want to look around? You have never bothered before. In fact, I do not think I have ever seen you go beyond the first floor,' she replies, handing her the keys, begrudgingly. 'If I were you I wouldn't go into the attic, if that is your thinking, as the floorboards up there are very dangerous.'

'That is very considerate of you, Kathy, but I am able to look after myself and, besides, it is time I took an interest in the old house.'

Kathy glares at Lizzy, who smiles smugly to herself, pleased to see her squirming, as she watches her scurry off, muttering, 'Never bothered herself with the house before, now all of a sudden she wants the run of it, stuck up bitch.'

'I am intrigued, why do you want the keys, Spud, Kathy is right, you have never taken an interest before?'

'Let's just say that this time I sense the old place is ready to yield up some of its secrets, which were not meant to be shared until this time.'

'First the church and now the house, is there nothing sacred in our lives any more?'

'Do not worry, honey, you are still its master.'

'Yeah, master of diddly-squat!' he groans, strutting off to Fagan and the freedom of the hills.

'What about us? What are we to do while you are wandering around this old mausoleum?' asks Robyn, eager to know what is in the attic now that Kathy has mentioned it.

'We treat this like any other case and so we start as we always do.'

'With the TIE, of course,' interrupts Sam, eager, like Robyn, to know more about the house, which is her dream country mansion that she could show off to her society friends back in London. She cannot understand

63

why Charity does not stay here more or why she does not like it. It is the perfect country retreat with its magnificent hallway, circular staircase in the centre and family portraits depicting the Holmes dynasty hanging from every available space. There are endless rooms leading off several floors and the large windows look out onto acres of land, all now belonging to Charity. Yes, she could easily see herself living here with Leo, who would be no less than a Lord of course, a fitting title to match such a grand house.

'Spot on, Sam, as usual you are ahead of me.'

'Thank you, old girl, and I think I should accompany you around the house. I would be your personal bodyguard, I mean Kathy could be right, these old mansions can be dangerous old places.'

'Oh yeah, as if you are going to fight them off single-handedly, I do not think so. You just want to nose around,' jokes Robyn.

'No I don't.'

'Now now, you two stop squabbling. I need you both; it is a big house and three pairs of eyes are better than one.'

'Yes,' shouts Sam excitedly, while Robyn is still chuckling away to herself.

'What about me, Miss Charity?' asks Jack, keen to do something other than just sitting around.

'I need to know the history of the village, Jack, everything you can dig up.'

'Old Mrs Simpson, she was born in the village and is a keen historian. She would be about eighty now, but still has a mind sharper than a razor. She would know everything there is to know about Grimoire.'

'Excellent.'

'Can I help you and the others check the house, my darling?'

'Sorry, Lizzy, but I need you to deal with the vicar. I do not want him in the church when we go there this afternoon. I do not know how you are going to do it, but he must not be there.'

'Why?'

'Because he is the guardian of the *Book of Shadows*, a warlock who hides behind the cloth of the church and who waits for the coming of the one who is destined to use its magic, the last descendant of the children of Lilith. If he destroys the last descendant, while they possess the book, then all their powers become his. He has waited centuries, changing disguises many times and knows the time is soon.'

'But surely this is a job for me, not Lizzy, it's far too dangerous. She would be better suited to my task and I to hers.'

'No, Jack, you are strong, but too easy to see through and he would know in seconds that I sent you. This requires the guile of a woman who can hide behind the layers of a woman's armour. It will take him longer to see through Lizzy, giving us precious time.'

'Do not worry, my darling, I will deal with this warlock. How dare he use the Lord's house for his evil.'

'Be careful, Lizzy, he is very powerful and has no soul, so exists only through others. I would not send you, but I have no choice. If he sees through you then call my name three times and I will hear you and come.'

'But that means he must have married you and Monty in the church if he has always been there!' says Robyn, thinking of all the times she has spoken to him over the years and yet her gift never *saw* him.

'Yes, but it is only now that I have the power to see all, dark and light, that I see who he truly is. I can see beyond the moment of time, so know that he is waiting. He has always known who I was, waiting for me to be reborn, so that I can claim what is mine as the last descendant. I must be cleverer than he if I am to possess the *Book of Shadows* before he sees me and returns.'

'How will you distract him, Lizzy?'

'I have not lived to this ripe old age without thinking on my feet many a times, Robyn, my darling, so do not fret, I will think of something.'

'Thanks, Lizzy, and remember, just say my name three times and I will come.'

'I will, my darling.'

'What do you want me to do? I know I am not an official member of the RING, but I cannot just sit back twiddling my thumbs,' says Leo, as Sam preens with pride.

'You do yourself a disservice, Leo. You are family, and as much a part of the RING as the rest of us, and I do need your help.'

'Yes, what is it that you want him to do?' shrieks Sam, unable to contain her excitement, as up until recently he never really got involved in her work with the RING, except for the occasional helping hand, usually at a distance and at her request. But now they are in the thick of it together, and how she loves it.

'I can speak for myself, darling, if you don't mind.'

'Sorry, couldn't help myself.'

Charity smiles as she looks at them, thinking how sweet they are together. The perfect match; she is like a bolt of lightning, injecting energy into an old staid soul, and he keeps her steady, protecting her from herself, that blind energy that sometimes leads her into trouble.

'Like Monty said, I have never really taken an interest in Holmes House, but now I must. Somewhere in the lineage of this house there is a link to my past and who I am, which is paramount to us completing our quest. I need you to find that link. You will see beyond the blindness of family. You will look with the eye of the judge, clinical and detached. You will see what others cannot.'

'But where do I start?'

'The library, it holds the key that will unlock the past of Holmes House.'

'You are very clever, Charity. You knew that Monty would want this task, but either felt that he would be too close to see or that he might find something that would upset him. You baited him with the keys to the house through Kathy, knowing that he would get upset and go off riding instead. You do not really need the keys do you?'

'No. I have a set already given to me by Mrs Holmes when I was helping to prepare for the wedding party. Then, when she asked for them back, I told her that I had lost them.'

'Why?' asks Robyn.

'I do not know why. I just had this overwhelming feeling that I needed to keep them.'

'It is that "no coincidences" thing again,' says Sam, rubbing her shoulders as she feels a chill running through her.

'But you are right about Monty possibly finding something that may upset him. I do not want that to happen, so would prefer you to do the checking, Leo.'

'No problem, consider it done.'

It is nine-thirty. Jack and Lizzy are the first to go, as they leave for the village, separately. Leo goes to his room to get his mini tape recorder, his essential piece of equipment whenever he needs to make notes, leaving the three of them making their way into the hallway.

The house feels too quiet, almost eerie, as they stand at the foot of the staircase looking up, while Monty's ancestors peer down upon them from their portraits, their eyes boring into them. As they look closer, they wonder where Monty gets his good looks from, because most of his forbears were ugly.

'I suppose you want to split up,' whispers Sam, suddenly losing all her curiosity.

'Some bodyguard,' jokes Robyn, moving closer to Charity, just in case.

'I have two sets of keys and I did say I needed three pairs of eyes, so who is going to go it alone?' asks Charity, teasing them, as they both look at each other.

'I think we should all stick together. After all, we have until lunch time and, besides, I have a feeling you know where to go anyway,' says Robyn.

'I see your gift is on top form today, and you are right, I know exactly what I am looking for and where it is.'

'Well don't keep us in suspense. What is it and where is it?' asks Sam, suddenly feeling much braver now that they are all going to be together.

'It's called the black mirror and it is in the attic.'

'I knew it, I knew it. It had to be the attic, especially when Kathy specifically told you not to go there. What is the black mirror? It sounds dangerous,' says Sam, trembling.

Robyn is exuberant; she knows of this mirror from stories as a child. 'It is used by witches for scrying,' she says.

'Scrying, what is that?' asks Sam.

'Shush,' whispers Charity, as they make their way up the stairs to the attic.

Sam feels her throat going dry, as the three of them stand, motionless, staring at a huge black door covered in cobwebs and spiders. 'It doesn't look like anybody has opened this door in a long time,' says Robyn, stepping back a couple of paces.

'You didn't finish telling me about the black mirror and scrying,' says Sam, suddenly feeling her legs turn to jelly.

'Scrying is when witches use an object to see the future and it is said that the black mirror has the power to show you this in its reflection, but it is a black reflection,' replies Charity, as she prepares to unlock the door.

'What do you mean, "black reflection", I do not think I like the sound of that?' says Sam, moving closer to her friends.

'It means we are looking into the future using black magic.'

'Black magic! Does that mean we could be in danger?' asks Sam, her voice suddenly rising a few octaves.

'Well it's not as friendly as white magic,' quips Robyn, who is just as scared, but is too curious not to look.

Charity unlocks the door, brushing aside the cobwebs, as Sam and Robyn follow close behind, clinging onto each other like Siamese twins.

'It is pitch black, and I cannot see a bloody thing. Shit, something has just brushed against my leg, and it is furry,' yells Sam.

'Stop panicking, you are even making me nervous, and I am too cool to be nervous,' says Robyn, as they fumble around in the dark.

'Too cool, now I have heard it all,' snaps Sam, as Charity finds a light switch and all becomes clear as they see the furry object: a dead rat.

'Ugh, I hate them, filthy things,' shrieks Sam, as she kicks it away.

They find themselves in the middle of the room, a dark, cold and damp place. It smells of death, the floor littered with furry corpses, mice, rats, a cat, flies and spiders, and a couple of small birds, all covered in cobwebs. The room is sparse with just a rickety old chair in the corner next to a broken single bed covered in moth-eaten sheets on top of a flea-ridden mattress. A dressing-table, eaten up by woodworm, is under the window with dusty, stained, torn curtains. There is a wardrobe falling to pieces in the corner and a mirror ... a five-foot free-standing oval mirror between the wardrobe and dressing-table.

The three of them huddle together, staring.

'It is totally black. There is no reflection. I cannot see myself. I cannot see anything in it,' says Sam, trembling.

'I have a bad feeling about this room, it reeks of death...'

'I know, Robyn, but I need to see the reflection in the mirror,' says Charity.

'Don't you mean we, we are in this together, aren't we?'

'Not the mirror. Sam and you must not see its reflection. Only I must call upon its magic.'

'Why?' asks Sam, nervously.

'To see the reflection of the future you must give a gift to the creature that lives in the mirror.'

'What creature? I don't see any creature.'

'It only comes when it is summoned and then you have to play the game.'

'What game?' asks Robyn.

'The food game,' replies Charity, as they suddenly notice that the room contains more corpses than furniture.

'The room is littered with dead bodies that are just shells, but not human. Does that mean we are safe?' asks Sam, timidly.

'Let's just say that they are the unfortunates who entered the room via other methods than the locked door, who then got a bit too close to the mirror,' says Charity.

'So what do we do now?' asks Sam.

'You must not be in front of the mirror when I call upon its magic. And should I not survive...'

'Hang on a second, did I hear the words "not survive",' Robyn says, panicking, when suddenly they hear a scratching noise coming from inside the mirror. They move closer to see. Something red is appearing, a small dot growing in the blackness, which, as it grows bigger, forms a shape like an hourglass. Out of the edges of the mirror grow thin black legs, eight of them, which curve around the glass.

'Who wishes to see into the mirror?' the voice asks, soft and inviting, a woman's voice, which hides a treacherous soul.

'I do,' replies Charity, moving forward, while pushing Robyn and Sam back.

'Come closer, my dear. Let me see who wishes to call upon the magic of the black mirror.'

'Don't go any closer,' shouts Sam, her body trembling.

Charity is not listening, as the mirror calls to her, inviting her into its soul.

'Ah pretty, very pretty. I like pretty things, they are so much sweeter than ugly creatures,' she says, as Charity looks deeper into the blackness, her body transfixed by the red hourglass.

'Now that we are nice and cosy together, what is it that you wish to see and what gift do you offer in return?'

'I wish to see my end and I offer you your favourite food,' she replies, as Robyn and Sam watch, open-mouthed.

'You are a brave pretty thing. Those who come seeking the black reflection of the future look for power, riches and glory, but none have wished to see their end. Why do you wish to know what others fear?'

'When I see the end I will know who I am, angel or demon.'

'We are what we are for that moment in time, but time does not stand still, and so the future can only be what the moment shows. Do you still wish to see?'

'I do.'

'Then let the game begin...'

The hourglass disappears and black becomes grey, as the mirror comes to life, and Charity sees a huge wall, separating two worlds. She is walking towards it, on a dark, misty path that seems endless, and as she draws closer, she sees two magnificent pillars supporting a glorious black iron gate. There are no locks or bolts on this gate, just beautiful carvings, which appear to move. The gate is alive, made up of living souls; it is the gate of penitent souls, who wait to cross over to the other side. The only way through is to touch it, and then you become it, trapped inside, awaiting the verdict of the one who decides your fate. What lies beyond the gate depends upon the moment of time, the time of final judgement...

Charity reaches out to touch it, but the vision disappears and she is back in the attic, standing in front of the mirror, looking into the red hourglass, which grows bigger. She is unable to move, transfixed by the glow of the hourglass when, suddenly, she is covered in an irregular, tangled web of coarse silk, a spider's web, which bursts forth from inside the mirror. She cannot move, as it comes towards her from out of the darkness of the mirror. It is a giant *Araneae Therididae*, the deadly black widow spider.

'Holy shit, look at the size of that! It must be at least seven foot,' screams Sam, as she and Robyn cower in the corner watching the spider tower over Charity, wrapping her in its web, repeatedly turning her with its eight huge legs, applying more and more silk until she's mummified alive inside it.

The spider looks at Charity, as she prepares to inject her with her venom, the kiss of death. One bite and the venom spreads rapidly through her body causing excruciating pain to her arms, legs, chest, back and abdomen, quickly followed by chills, abdominal cramps, spasms, vomiting, profuse perspiration, delirium and finally paralysis. Sam and Robyn watch in horror, helpless, as the spider prepares to suck the body fluids from her, culminating by discarding her carcass on the floor with the others.

'I don't know what to do! What do we do?' cries Sam, as they watch the spider bend down, eyeballing Charity.

'It has been a long time since I have had the pleasure of such sweet meat, how delicious this moment is going to be.'

Charity is trapped, unable to move, as the paralysis takes grip, preventing her from shape-shifting her way out. She is doomed. She feels the touch of the spider's kiss upon her face.

Suddenly, she hears a voice inside her head, it's Robyn calling to her through the power of infallible thought. 'How can I stop it? What do I do, Charity?' Although her body is failing, her mind is still strong, as she replies, 'Break the mirror, Robyn, break it now, hurry.'

Robyn moves swiftly, running towards the mirror. The spider spots her and leaves Charity to protect it, but Robyn is too quick. She picks up the chair, smashing it into the mirror, shattering it into hundreds of pieces of black glass, which fly through the air towards the spider, who desperately tries to escape the flying missiles of broken glass, but it's not quick enough, as the glass penetrates its body.

As each piece of glass cuts into it, the mirror is sucked along, slowly disappearing into the spider until its body becomes the mirror, expanding until it explodes into a thousand pieces of blackness, which disappear into the air, releasing Charity, as the web disintegrates, and she feels her body returning, and the arms of her friends around her.

10

Defixiones

They lock the door behind them, running down the stairs without looking back, until they reach the library, where Leo is sitting at a desk under the bay window surrounded by mounds of books and paper.

'What has happened? You look as if you have just seen a ghost,' he says, as they collapse on the couch.

'Worse than that, Charity was nearly eaten alive by a seven foot black widow spider,' says Sam, breathlessly, trying to regain her composure.

'A seven foot spider, really?'

'Yes really. Ask them if you do not believe me.'

Leo listens, open-mouthed, as Robyn relays the story.

'But how did you know that this black mirror and spider were in the attic?' he asks.

'When Kathy told me not to go there, then I knew where to look,' says Charity.

'Ah ha, I knew it, she is a bad lot, I could see it in her eyes, small squinty little things.'

'No, it is not what you think, Sam, she was protecting me. She has kept that room locked for twenty years, ever since her beloved dog, Ben, wandered in there and came across the spider. She saw him eaten and the spider return to the mirror, but never told anyone about it.'

'Why?' asks Robyn.

'She could not believe what she was seeing, but at the same time knew that it had happened. How would she explain such a thing to Mr and Mrs Holmes? She was terrified that they would dismiss her, so has kept the secret of the black mirror hidden all these years, telling everyone that the floorboards in the room were dangerous and that the room was too far away in the house to be of any use, and so it remained locked.'

'How did she explain the dog?' asks Sam.

'She said it wandered into the stables and got kicked by one of the horses when he got too close, and she buried him in the fields.'

'But how do you know all this if she told no one?' asks Leo. 'What was the mirror doing in the attic in the first place and how come you needed to look into it?'

'Yeah, and what did you see?' asks Sam, her curiosity back in full swing.

'Since my battle with Lucifer at the Court of Past Souls, where I was nearly lost to the underworld, I feel different, stronger and more powerful. I seem to know things. I hear voices telling me what to do and where to look and I see visions, showing me places and people that I have never met, yet I seem to know them, like the warlock, and the black mirror. I do not always understand the reasons behind these revelations or what connection they have to me. I have no control over them. I just know that I must follow whatever path they show. The warlock is clear, he is my enemy and I have been forewarned, but the mirror I do not understand, except to say that I had to look into it.'

'But why, what was so important that you risked your life?' Robyn asks.

'I still do not know who I am? These powerful forces are growing within me, taking me over, changing me into something else. I am afraid that when I am finally united with my other soul, the dark one, and become the power of two and the definitive battle with evil begins...'

They feel her anguish, as Robyn holds her tight. 'It will be OK. You will be OK.'

Charity looks into her eyes. 'I am not sure. I fear that my final nemesis will...'

'Stop, you are scaring me. Nothing bad is going to happen to you. You always win. Have we not beaten every evil demon and creature that that ugly horned goat of whatever has sent, and we will destroy him,' yells Sam, desperately trying to be brave for her friend, when inside she is crumbling.

'That is the point, Sam, he cannot be destroyed. You cannot kill what does not live. At best we can only stop him, but he will just come back and back and back until he wins.'

'What are you saying? That we are all wasting our time and that we might as well give up now. What did you really see in the mirror? Because, according to Lizzy, you are the one that everyone has been waiting for, the one that can destroy him, so why are you so afraid?' asks Leo, trembling with anger and fear, anger at Charity for taking them on a quest to fight a battle that is hopeless and fear at the very thought of that hopelessness.

'Forgive me, Leo, you are right. We cannot just give in to evil; our world would not exist at all if we did not continue the battle. I am not afraid of the battle, but of myself. I saw a gate, a living gate, called the gate of the penitent souls. This gate is where my soul is destined to end, but I could not see what was on the other side. I could not see whether it was darkness or light, whether I become the very demon that I was born to destroy. I see many things, but I cannot see that, the one thing I wish to see the most.'

'But why are you so afraid? You are the Inceptor with the power of the angels within you. You are the light.'

'Do you not see, Robyn, Lizzy's words say it all. I shall become the dark to fight the dark. I am the last and the last will perish, but darkness cannot be accepted into the afterlife, so where does my soul go?'

There is that chilling feeling of suppressed panic in the air, as they ask themselves the same question. What if Charity's fear is real, what becomes of them?

'You still did not explain how the mirror ended up in the attic?' asks Sam, trying to escape her dark thoughts.

Charity pulls herself back from the vision of the living gate, locking it deep in her subconscious, knowing that it will resurrect itself when the time comes.

'This house has a dark history, which I suspect involved witchcraft and pagan rituals, and I am certain now that some of Monty's forbears were followers of Satanism. The black mirror is Satan's doorway to the underworld and his familiars, demons in animal form, who assisted witches in the casting of spells, often used to destroy their enemies. They probably used the mirror to see into the future and then cast spells upon those they wished to harm using black magic. They would have to offer a sacrifice to the familiar; in this case the black widow spider, in return for their lives once they had looked into its reflection. They would entice innocents into the house and then show them the mirror, offering them the chance to look into the future. Unaware of their fate, they would not be able to resist, but their only future was the kiss of death, from the black widow spider.'

'Do you think Monty knows about the mirror and his ancestors' dark past?' asks Robyn.

'He must know, he works for the government in Special Operations. It is his job to find things out, besides, people talk in small country villages like Grimoire; gossip is rife

77

and secrets will always out in the end,' says Sam, suddenly wondering if she really knows Monty at all, this kind, gentle man who would lay down his life for his friends, yet can be so brutally cold towards his enemies. For the first time she sees a dark side to him, the side she always thought of as a warrior, but maybe he has more of the beast in him than she thought.

Charity always felt that Monty knew more about his ancestors' sadistic past than he let on, but he is not like them, he has a good soul and she knows that whatever secrets he has kept were to protect her. His constant fear that there was someone or something dark lurking in the shadows, watching them and waiting. Now she understands why he is so protective of her and why their souls touched when they met. They were always destined to be together. He is the link between the lineage of Holmes House and her past. He knew that one day she would uncover its unholy secrets. Through him she will find the vacuous spirit and her other soul.

There are no coincidences...

She turns to Leo. 'What have you discovered?' she asks, hesitantly, afraid of what he is about to reveal.

'It is fascinating stuff and you were right about the link, which I believe I have found,' he says excitedly.

'I knew you would, darling,' squeals Sam, bursting with pride.

'You were almost right about the mirror and witchcraft. I uncovered the original deeds to the house, which were locked away in a hidden room that I found accidentally when I fell against the wall while carrying a pile of books.'

'A secret room, fabulous, where is it?' shouts Sam, leaping off the chair.

'Over here, but I warn you it is not a room to dwell in too long. I felt something in there, watching me, when I was going through the papers. I could not stay there;

it is an evil place. So I grabbed as much as I could and left.'

They enter the room, which is completely red. Red walls, red floor, red candles, red curtains, and a large red table in the middle with a black circle painted in the centre, upon which lie two black *defixiones* made of lead, with writing on them, in what looks like dried blood. Beside the *defixiones* lie a black-handled athame and a quill made from the feathers of a raven.

'*Defixiones* used by black witches and warlocks,' says Robyn, whispering and staying close to Charity, as the evil in the room is so pungent it almost makes her heave.

'What are *defixiones*? Although I have a feeling I know the answer,' asks Sam, clinging onto Leo, who, like the others, can feel a malevolent presence all around them.

'It is Latin for curse tablets, which were used in the ancient world from the sixth century BC onward to 'bind' the enemy or opponent by means of a curse. It had to be in the blood of the witch or warlock casting it for it to work. They would cut their wrist with the athame, drawing blood, and then write the curse on the tablet with the quill, executed within ten minutes of drawing blood, so that the blood was still warm when casting the curse. The ritual had to be performed in the magic circle known as the sacred area, while casting the spell and chanting aloud three times. When the blood was cold and dried indelibly into the tablet, then the curse was set and the victim's fate sealed. The curse was irreversible once cast,' says Charity.

'I call...'

'Do not say it, Sam, to speak the words aloud is to evoke the one who wrote it,' shouts Robyn, as they all freeze, huddled together in this unholy of places, their eyes darting everywhere. Charity moves closer to the tablets.

The first tablet:

> *I call upon the four elements*
> *to give power and strength to thy spell.*
> *I summon the spirits of eternal damnation,*
> *and offer thy blood to seal this curse.*
>
> ♀
>
> *Let the sins of thy self descend upon he who turns*
> *away.*

The second tablet:

> *I cast this spell in the name of thy Lord.*
> *I call upon his soldiers to quell she who is last,*
> *let thy blood be the strewing of he who comes.*
> *Seventy-seven be the sign to annihilation of the three,*
>
> ♀
>
> *and he will devour the sun.*

The room is silent. Charity pulls herself back from the tablets. 'We must leave this place now.'

'Why? What do you see?' asks Robyn.

'I do not see it, I feel it. It is in the walls, the floors, and its very fabric. The room is possessed, cursed by those who cast the spell. We must leave now or there will be no escape.'

They turn quickly and make their way to the door, but it is too late, there is no door. They rush to the curtains, but there are no windows, and no way out; the room has entombed them.

'Oh, God, what are we going to do? We will die in here. I cannot breathe,' screams Sam, as Leo desperately tries to calm her, while Robyn and Charity are channelling their powers.

'There must be a way out,' yells Robyn, 'but I cannot

see it, my gift is not strong enough. What can we do? The room seems impenetrable. Sam is right, we are doomed...'

Charity is silent, as she paces the room like a caged animal, looking around her, sniffing the air, smelling the stench of death that seeps through the walls into their skin. She has never been in such an unholy place. It is the nucleus of the Antichrist, where his soldiers gathered to worship their leader and do his bidding. The room is laughing at them, as it sucks the goodness from their bodies, slowly, until their souls seep into its very fabric, becoming the spirits of eternal damnation.

'I cannot die here, not this place. Please, Charity, do something,' cries Sam, as Leo cradles her in his arms, while Robyn looks at Charity, waiting.

Charity picks up the athame in her right hand, drawing blood from her left, while holding it over the tablets. Her warm blood drips slowly onto them. Loudly, she recites:

'I call upon the four elements,
to give power and strength to thy spell.
I summon thy mother Hecate – triple goddess of the underworld,
and offer thy blood to seal this curse.
♀
Let thy blood be the slaying of the damned.

There is a moment of condemned silence, as Charity and the RING wait.

Then it happens...

The tablets rise up from the table, floating in the air, as the room quakes all around them. The walls begin to crumble, suddenly; the tablets explode into thousands of tiny pieces forming the sign of the Antichrist ‡ in the

81

air. They move towards Charity and before she breathes her next breath, they enter her mouth, consuming her, her body shaking violently before collapsing to the floor, as dark now overshadows them, and the room is no more.

'Are you all right? Please God let her be OK.'

'I am fine, just fine,' she replies, as Sam helps her up from the floor, crying. 'There is no need for tears, Sam, they only make your eyes puffy and you know how you hate that,' she says gently, smiling.

'I am sorry, Charity, forgive me. I lost the plot and now you have swallowed the tablets and their curse,' cries Sam.

'I eat curses for breakfast,' she jokes, but underneath she knows that there will be a price to pay for destroying Satan's den.

'How did we end up back in the library? And the room, it has just disappeared!' says Leo in a daze.

'I would not even go there, darling, as Lizzy is always saying, the world of spirits moves in its own mysterious way,' says Sam, smiling at Charity, a true friend indeed.

'Why did you pull back from the tablets? What did you see in them?' asks Robyn, suspecting that the curse on the tablets has something to do with Charity and the coming of the King of Terror.

She is quiet, the tablets are the sign. They are getting closer, but the curse has already been set, and is irreversible. It is inside her now, where its power will become even more potent, but she had no choice. To let her friends die and their souls be damned forever, or use her powers to save them? She knew that by destroying the room, its magic would become stronger, as it now lives within her – the host it was seeking. She has won nothing, only time, but at what cost?

She must be careful. She knows the meaning of the first tablet, but the second is still a puzzle, yet she is sure of one thing, that it is the clue to the one she is seeking, the Antichrist who will devour the sun. What does she tell her friends? She cannot hide the truth from them or Monty, but it is not the time to reveal all, she must be economical with her translation.

'What did you see, Charity?' asks Robyn, assertively.

'The two tablets are connected. The first tablet is a hex.'

'What is that?' asks Sam.

'An evil spell made against another to do them harm.'

'Who is it?' shouts Sam.

'Well if you stop interrupting then she might be able to tell us,' says Robyn, exasperated.

'The black witch or warlock who cast the hex offered his or herself to its master in return for immortality, but if the hex is broken then he or she will be damned in the victim's place. The victim...' she cannot speak.

'It is Monty; he is the one who turns away?' says Robyn, quietly.

'Yes,' she replies, the words choking her. 'He does not follow his forbears' path; he is an innocent in the ways of Satanism, but whoever cast the hex could see that our paths were meant to cross, and so, through Monty, their black magic lives on.'

'How do you mean through Monty?' asks Leo.

'Monty does not know it, but they will use him to get to me. He must not know this. You must not tell him,' she pleads.

'Why not?' he asks. 'If he knows then he is prepared, otherwise...'

'No, he must not know of this hex against him. It will destroy him if he thinks our union was born out of darkness.'

'But it was. The curse tablet shows that. It is no coincidence that you were meant to meet; he has the darkness within him.'

'No he has not,' she yells, ashamed that Robyn could even think such a thing let alone say it aloud. 'He carries the curse, but he is not his ancestors. The creature that cast the hex in his master's likeness is the one we should be seeking. Monty is blameless and without sin against his soul; he is a pure being. Understand this; if you tell him of the curse tablet and what happened today in Satan's den, it will be our undoing.'

'What do we do then?' asks Robyn.

'Nothing, the curse is within me now.'

'So what about Monty, does that mean he no longer carries the hex?'

'It is not that simple, Robyn. I destroyed the tablets, but not the curse, it lives on through me, but I still do not know how or when it will come; only that Monty will be the instrument of its beginning.'

'But does that mean the end of you and Monty?' asks Robyn.

'Never ever say that again,' she says angrily. 'Monty and I are two halves of the same soul and always will be. Whatever dark magic appeared in that room it will not destroy us. I will fight them. They will not have him. They will not have us.'

'Here you all are, and what has my intrepid team been up to in my absence?' Monty asks, bounding in full of life after his ride.

No one speaks. 'What is going on? Why are you all staring at me? What has happened?' he asks, suddenly feeling a coolness in the air, the kind of 'cannot put your finger on it, but something is very wrong' type of coolness.

'Nothing is going on, honey; we were just discussing what Leo has found.'

'Judging by the look on all your faces it has got to be something to do with the house and its secrets. Well I love hearing about secrets so cough up, what have you uncovered?'

84

Leo freezes, terrified to say anything, while looking over at Charity, as the others try to act nonchalant, but it is obvious that something is not right.

'OK, now I know something is wrong so you had better tell me before...'

'We found a curse tablet,' interrupts Charity quickly.

'What tablet?'

'A curse tablet, it's when a spell is written in blood.'

'Oh that kind of tablet, so what has this tablet to do with Holmes House?'

No one utters a word, as they all look to Charity, who knows she must tell him something, but not everything, especially the curse on the first tablet.

'I hate to tell you this honey, but it appears that some of your ancestors practised witchcraft and worshipped Satan.'

They waited with bated breath, as he froze, and then said, 'I know.'

'You knew and said nothing,' she says angrily, as Robyn chips in.

'Why keep it a secret? We have no secrets from each other.'

Charity cannot understand why her gift of clear seeing failed her and why she did not see anything, until today. Why today? She did not see into Monty's soul or Holmes House, except that she felt it was a sinister place. A house with secrets, which she hated the moment she set foot inside it.

The second tablet – now she sees...

'Do not get angry, Spud, it is just that if your ancestors' past was as depraved as mine, wouldn't you want to keep quiet about it?'

'It is OK, honey, I see it now.'

'You do?' asks Robyn.

'The tablet, it is a curse against the heretics.' She is

careful to refer to the second tablet as the only one, protecting Monty. 'Centuries ago there was a witch craze in the village, when the church burnt all the witches and warlocks in the main town for all to witness, some of whom were Monty's ancestors. In revenge, they placed a curse against the church, the village and all those born into the Holmes family who did not follow the path of Satanism. The curse tablet called upon the soldiers of the Antichrist to quell she who is last.'

'She who is last – that is you, Spud!' says Monty, suddenly feeling those dark forces around him again.

'The first part of the curse was to blind she ... me ... from the truth. So whenever I came here I felt something, but I could not see it. Their magic was too powerful and my powers weak, but now I see it all, as I become as powerful as they, and that is what they fear.'

'You said the first part,' exclaims Sam, clutching Leo tightly.

'The second part is about the annihilation of the three: the vacuous spirit, my other soul and me, where seventy-seven will be the sign. They must destroy the three so that he can come – the King of Terror. The Antichrist in human form. He will bring with him death, which will spread like a plague throughout the earth, devouring all that it touches, until the light is obliterated and the prophesy – he who will devour the sun – has been fulfilled, and the new millennium of darkness begins.'

'Can you see who he is?' asks Monty.

'No.'

'The deeds, it is in the deeds. That is where you will see the sign that you are looking for,' shouts Leo, excitedly.

'What do you mean?' asks Charity, her heart beating fast.

'The name and address on the original deeds – it is not Holmes House. It was originally called Quatrain House, number seventy-seven Quatrain House...'

86

'Nostradamus,' whispers Charity. 'Well done, Leo, I knew you would find it.'

'Oh my God, you are right, the prophecies,' yells Robyn.

'I do not understand, Spud. How do you leap from the deeds to my house to Nostradamus?' asks Monty, totally confused.

'The name, the sign is in the name, Quatrain House,' she replies.

'I am with Monty on this one, I am totally lost,' says Sam.

'Nostradamus was one of the world's most famous prophets. He was born in the early sixteenth century and predicted events into the third millennium. He wrote his predictions in four line rhyming verse called quatrains, which were cryptic codes concealing his true predictions about future events. These quatrains were organised into groups of one hundred, which he called a century, but he did not always complete each century, for example, one century only had forty-two quatrains in it. He completed nine hundred and forty-two quatrains, one of which was *Quatrain 77 – Century VIII*, which read:

> *The Antichrist very soon annihilates the three;*
> *Seven and twenty years his war will endure,*
> *The heretics are dead, imprisoned, exiled,*
> *Red hail, water, blood and corpses cover the earth.*

'The quatrains are so cryptic that whoever reads them can put their own interpretation upon them, but there is no denying that many of his prophecies have since been fulfilled.'

'What does *Quatrain 77* predict?' asks Leo, nervously.

'Take your pick from the many interpretations by learned scholars, mathematicians, scientists et cetera, but they all seem to agree on one thing, that he is referring to the early years of the new millennium. One of the interpretations, according to traditional Christian beliefs, is that he predicted the coming of the Antichrist, also known as the King of Terror. He will come in the guise of a false saviour, who is really the Prince of Hell, the Devil's advocate, who will wreak havoc in the world and lead much of humanity into the paths of damnation. Then begins the one thousand years of darkness...'

11

The Book of Shadows

Monty's mobile rings, it's Jack. 'I'll meet you outside the church, I'm still with Mrs Simpson.'

'OK, see you in thirty minutes.'

'Who was that?' asks Charity.

'Jack. He will meet us at the church. Getting back to the curse against the village, church and us, how does it work?'

'I do not understand it in its entirety yet,' she replies, trying to avoid the first tablet and the curse against Monty. 'But part of the curse has already been fulfilled.'

'Which part?'

'The vicar or should I say warlock and the village, the secrets of which lie hidden with old Mrs Simpson...'

'What about the curse against us?'

Charity hesitates, but Leo comes to her rescue. 'No worries there, Charity eats curses for breakfast and you and Jack annihilate them before dinner, besides, they did not reckon on having the RING to deal with.'

Everyone laughs, but it is a false laugh, while Robyn tries to deflect Monty's question back to the quatrain.

'Who is this Antichrist? According to *Quatrain 77*, he will be coming in our time and in the guise of a false saviour.'

'In Nostradamus's quatrains he tells of three powerful

and tyrannical leaders, whom he called the Antichrists, who would arise and seduce the people with promises of greatness, and once the people were theirs, the reign of terror would begin. The first of the Antichrists was decoded as Napoleon, and the second, Adolf Hitler.'

'Who is the third?' asks Sam.

'I cannot see that yet, but in the quatrain Nostradamus predicts that when he comes the skies will bleed with blood followed by twenty-seven years of war before the darkness.'

'Now that you have found the sign, *Quatrain 77*, where do we go from here?' asks Monty.

'The *Book of Shadows*, I must get the book, it will show me the way.'

'What about the vicar? And we haven't heard from Lizzy?' asks Robyn, worried.

'We will know soon enough when we get to the church,' says Charity.

'Where is Jack?' asks Monty, as they stand outside the church.

'How are we going to get in? The gates are locked,' says Robyn.

Charity touches the gates, they open, no one speaks. Then Jack turns up. 'Great the gates aren't locked,' he says, while everyone is silent, numb at Charity's new powers, which grow more amazing by the hour.

'What did you find out at Mrs Simpson's?' asks Sam, eagerly.

'No time for that now,' says Charity, as they make their way up the path, past the gravestones to a locked solid wood oval door. No one moves or says a word, they just wait, as Charity opens the door with a gentle touch of her hand.

They step into the outer vestibule and feel the coldness seep into their souls; this is not a holy place, but something else. Monty and Charity look at each other, their faces wretched with the thought that their union was blessed in this den of evil, and that the curse, placed by the shape-shifting warlock in the guise of the vicar, was cast upon them on that day.

Slowly they make their way down the aisle, which was once a bright haven of tranquillity, but now they see its true self, the house of Satan.

They gaze up at the cross hanging directly above the centre of the altar, their Lord, the one true being, but, as they look closer, they see that he is not the same, that this is not their God. Where there was sacrifice and love in his eyes, they see depravity and where there was forgiveness and peace in his face, they see suffering and damnation. How could they not have seen this before? Their bodies go cold as they wrap themselves in their arms, feeling the feverish chill of death pass over them.

'The sooner we are out of this place the better,' says Sam, shivering.

'But how do we find the book?' asks Jack.

'It is buried deep underground, hidden in the tomb of the damned,' says Charity.

'Not again, we always end up in the company of corpses,' moans Sam.

'Where is this tomb, Spud?' asks Monty, squeezing her hand tightly, trying desperately to hold onto her before ... he cannot, will not, think of losing her.

'It is in the crypt under the church.'

'Of course, it has to be the darkest, creepiest place.'

'Stop whingeing Sam,' says Robyn, who unlike her dear friend, is fearless and eager to see what is below.

'I suppose your new powers have shown you where it is?'

'You're reading my mind again, honey,' she jokes, leading them behind the alter to a door, which leads them down a long, winding, damp stone staircase that opens up into a large cavern lit by thirteen candles placed in a circle on the walls. In the centre, cemented into the ground, is a large stone coffin.

They circle the coffin, and as they draw closer they see a large cross cut into it ... the sign of the Antichrist ⸸.

'Who the hell is buried here?' asks Jack, as the others stare at him in horror.

'Do you see who is in the coffin, Spud?'

'It is the warlock's original body, his shell, and unfortunately the book is buried with him.'

'Why?' asks Leo.

'He is its guardian. He knows that I must open the coffin to get to the book and that is when he will come. We do not have much time. Once he is here, he will try to possess the book by destroying me, taking my essence, and placing my shell of a body in the coffin instead of his. He will use his new powers to re-enter his earthly body, making him all-powerful and giving him the power to be whatever he chooses – beast or man. He will be immortal, devouring all that he touches, and his appetite for fresh souls for his master will be unquenchable. He can leave this place and move amongst us, shape-shifting into any person or beast that he chooses to possess, living their lives, destroying all that comes within his path, and then when he has sucked every last drop of goodness from them, he moves on to another, and another, and so on until there are no more.'

'But he is already living amongst us,' says Sam, moving further and further away from the coffin.

'Yes, but he cannot leave Grimoire or take another soul, only the vicars who come to run the church. He is the guardian of the book, waiting for the last – me – to come so that he can be free. The price he was willing to pay for immortality. He gave his soul to the Devil in return for the promise of immortal power and so he waits, patiently, for that day, today...'

'So he was once mortal like us?'

'A long, long time ago, Sam, but he worshipped the Lord of Darkness and wished for more than his earthly powers. He is a very powerful witch and we must be careful if we are to win.'

They stand, staring at the cross, edged deep into the coffin, wondering how they are going to open it and get to the book before its guardian knows they are there.

'The stone is too heavy for us to move,' says Jack, as they all attempt to push it open.

'I must call upon the warlock's black magic,' says Charity, looking worried.

'What happens then?' asks Robyn, sensing her fear.

'He will know and come swiftly, through the magic of the shape-shifter, to protect it, but I have no choice.'

She steps back from the coffin, indicating to the RING to form an outer circle around it, but as they make the sphere between the two worlds, spirit and mortal, they feel a cold wind, as the candles flicker and the whispers of the gods touch them in the darkness of the crypt. She must open the circle with the four elements – air, fire, water, and earth – by using them to seal the four corners, protecting the inner circle, where she, the charge, will perform the invocation, inviting a spirit into her body by saying the words of evocation. She reaches into her pocket and brings out four tarot cards, sword, wand, cups and pentacle. Each symbol corresponds to the four elements: air to the east, fire to the south, water to the west, and earth to the north. She places them in the four corners, thus protecting the inner circle.

Now she is ready to call upon the spirits, inviting them into her sacred space, the inner circle, herself...

Lizzy is with the vicar five miles outside the village in another church, St Michael's, where he has come, at her request, to help her come to terms with the past. He is uncomfortable, as they sit in the pews with the sun shining down upon them through the beautiful stained-glass window that dominates the aisle. Painted into the glass is a magnificent portrait of Archangel Michael, her protector, and the reason she chose this church, where she would be safe. This is consecrated ground, unlike his unholy church, and he is the weak one here, but he knows that Lizzy could lead him to Charity.

She had to think of something to get him far enough away from his church to give Charity enough time, and so she tempted him with her pleas of guilt, entreating him with her desire to confess, knowing that he would not be able to resist.

'Thank you for coming here today, father, and I hope you do not mind hearing my confession in another church, but like I told you on the telephone, I did not want anybody to see me coming to your church in case it got back to my family.'

'Do not worry, Mrs?'

'Just call me Lizzy, father, everyone does.'

'Lizzy, I am here for you, just take your time and know that God is an understanding father,' he says in that creepy, treacherous tone of his, which she never really noticed before until Charity unmasked him. She looks him over, as he sits there, playing the dutiful vicar, with his portly body, fat face with no neck and balding shiny head, which he keeps wiping with a filthy hanky. There is a pungent smell coming from him that she always

94

thought was a bad case of BO, but now she knows different. Charity would often say that evil spirits have a sickly smell seeping from them, so if you ever come across a mortal with that very same smell, then beware...

Lizzy has a secret, which he knows will destroy Charity, but how will he get her to reveal it, the cat and the mouse. Which one will win? The game of wits begins.

'I can see you are troubled, Lizzy, but unless you unburden yourself I cannot offer you penance and God's forgiveness.'

'It is difficult, father,' she says, trying to hold him without giving anything away, but inside she needs to tell her secret. If only he was a real priest then she could release herself of this burden, but he is not. Yet she is in the house of God, and the compulsion to confess grows more urgent.

He feels her need.

'You are in great pain, Lizzy, because the secret you carry is wrong. It is a lie. A lie that you have nurtured for too many years, which you must release, otherwise damnation will be your final fate.'

'No, father,' she cries, forgetting for a moment who he really is, as he feeds on her guilt and fear of her own worthlessness.

'How can God accept you into His kingdom when your soul is tainted with a lie? You must cleanse yourself before Him, in His house, only then will all be right in His eyes,' he says, cupping her hands in his, feeding her fear, as she sees herself burning in the fires of hell.

'I did not do wrong, father. I had no choice. I did it to protect my girls. Is it wrong to protect the ones you love,' she says, crying.

'No it is not, but it is wrong to hold onto a lie. Unburden your soul to God and know peace,' he says, smiling, knowing that he has her...

95

'I...' she stops, realising what power she is about to give to the Devil's disciple.

His poky little eyes light up. He is almost there... soon he will hold the key to lure Charity to the crypt, where he can destroy her and finally possess the *Book of Shadows*, which...

He hears Charity saying the words of evocation... 'You think to trick me, how stupid you really are, you silly old woman.'

'Not that silly, you devil worshipper,' she retorts. 'You came didn't you?' she says defiantly.

He stands up, his portly body metamorphosing before her, as he shape-shifts into the bird of swiftness, the devil-falcon. It towers over her, spreading its huge wings, as she looks up, gulping, at the hideous beast before her, part bird, part devil, with its ugly goat's head and inverted horns, red eyes and tail.

He laughs. 'Get ready to enter the kingdom of thy Lord, Lizzy,' he says, as she sees his devil head coming towards her, and feels the breath of eternal damnation upon her face. The moment is upon her, as she closes her eyes and whispers, 'Charity, Charity, Charity...'

Charity stops; Lizzy's words ring in her ears as she sees her beloved aunt in trouble.

'What is it, Charity? What do you see?' asks Robyn.

'It's Lizzy, he knows.'

'Oh my God, what do we do?'

'Close your eyes, Robyn and see. See for all your worth,' she says, as the two of them fuse their minds together, becoming one, where they are transported to the chapel to see the devil-falcon about to strike. 'The window, Robyn, look at the window,' she shouts, as the two of them focus on the archangel, whose light beams down upon them.

'I call upon thy Lord
to breathe life into his likeness
send forth your soldier of the heavens
to defend thy servant.'

Charity's words are carried by the spirits, through the winds, into the church, shattering the stained-glass window, as the archangel comes to life, and the falcon turns to see his enemy flying towards him in a blaze of light, blinding him as he wields his sword of justice, while Lizzy marvels at the wondrous vision before her.

The two are eye-to-eye, as they hover above the aisle, their wings spread wide, eclipsing the church, with the light filtering through their feathers forming rays of heavenly beams, which strike into the core of God's house.

'Her powers have become awesome in her awakening, but without the book she cannot possess the power of two,' the falcon screeches, as the archangel floats before him, unforgiving in his champion of Lizzy.

'You enter the house of thy Lord with treachery in your soul and now you must choose; fight or flight.'

The devil-falcon rears his ugly head, as he realises that he cannot win the war, even if he wins the battle. Stay and fight, and maybe Lizzy's soul will be his. However, Charity will have the book.

Failure is not acceptable in his Lord's kingdom. If he concedes to this battle, but wins the next, destroying Charity, then, he will be the all-powerful one.

'Take her; her soul is less than worthless to thy Lord,' he says, swooping down and hovering over her, as she stares straight into him, fearless. 'There will be another day of reckoning, Lizzy.'

He spins around, flying up to face his adversary, his eyes burning with hatred, but the desire for immortality and the fear of failure before his master is greater. He flaps his magnificent wings and takes flight.

'She is safe,' cries Charity.

'But he is coming,' shouts Robyn, as she sees, through her third-eye, the devil-falcon flying through the skies towards them...

Charity looks to the four corners, beginning the evocation, inviting the spirits of the four elements – Eurius, air; Notus, fire; Zephyrus, water; and Boreas, earth – into the four cardinal points.

> *'Blessed be thee,*
> *I call upon the four spirits of the gods*
> *to rise up from their watchtowers*
> *and give life to she who is last.*
> *Destroy he who covets the magic of Grimoire;*
> *Blessed be thee.'*

The wind howls and the spirits scream, as the RING draw breath, feeling the earth erupting beneath them, while Charity waits...

They rise up from the ashes. East, Eurius, Lord of Air, the handsome youth; South, Notus, Lord of Fire, the young warrior; West, Zephyrus, Lord of Water, the middle-aged man; and finally, North, Boreas, Lord of the Earth, the wise old man. Four Gods for four elements and the four stages of man. The four cardinal points are sealed, protecting the inner circle, Charity's sacred space, as the RING, in the outer circle, completes the invocation.

'We meet again, Charity,' says Zephyrus, glowing in his white robes of the gods.

Charity salutes the gods, one by one, as they stand erect at each cardinal point. Glorious in robes of white silk, while holding their sceptres of the four elements in their right hands. 'I greet you, Eurius, Notus, Zephyrus and Boreas, as your humble servant, and call upon your ancient powers to release the *Book of Shadows* to I, she who is last, so that the prophesied *Quatrain 77* be fulfilled.'

Boreas, the father of wisdom, strokes his long white beard. He speaks in the tongue of shamanic verse. 'The sacred decree of the Druids has been fulfilled, as prophesied by the gods, where this day the *Book of Grimoire* will be the instrument in the rebirth of the two.'

The gods of the ancient world of magic raise their hands in the air, commanding the four elements. The winds howl, while the flames of eternal life erupt around the RING, who stand frigid with consternation in the outer circle, as the waters cascade over Charity, baptising her with the power of the gods. The earth rises up from beneath them, elevating them high above the coffin, which, as they look down upon it, begins to open, revealing the warlock's soulless shell, under which lies *Grimoire*, the *Book of Shadows*.

The crypt is a magical world, coming alive with the flames of eternal life. The gods' luminous light blinds the RING with its purity, while the waters of the heavens cascade over Charity, who bathes in the reflective glory of her ancestors, immersing herself in their radiance, as the powerful shamanic magic reignites itself through the all-seeing eyes of the gods. Four bolts of lightning strike through her body, the forehead, the eyes, the mouth and finally the soul, liberating her from the constraints of her earthly self; exalting her into the world of the supernatural being...

Boreas, Lord of the Earth, calls to the book:

'By the powers of the four elements,
we the watchtowers of the ancient laws,

command the spirits of Grimoire
to arise from the shadows
♀
and become one
with she who is last.'

The corpse rises up from the pit of Satan ... followed by the book ... floating towards Charity, who reaches out to...

'The book is mine. Come to me thy sacred Grimoire.'

The vileness of the words ricochets around the crypt, as the book stops in mid air, and the wings of the devil-falcon descend upon them, blowing out the candles, as they feel the black magic of the underworld cast its darkness over them.

'Stay, I command thee,' she says. 'Let those whose healing magic created thee in their likeness and whose spirits live within I, she who is last, and thee, be thy true masters.'

She is face to face with the Devil's soldier, divided by his shell and the book, two opposing worlds seeking the eternal magic of *Grimoire*. He spreads his wings, preparing for battle, as the gods watch, unable to interfere, for only two can fight for possession of *Grimoire*, the guardian and the last descendant, but only one can survive. The RING pray, as the gods are silent, waiting for the book's return to the last descendant, Charity, and the prophecy fulfilled.

'We do not have to fight,' she says, offering him the chance of absolution.

'Only the weak offer defeat before the battle has begun,' he retorts, as he calls upon the dark magic of his Lord.

'Come and get it,' she says, calmly.

A black storm erupts, as the RING and the gods feel the chilling touch of evil against their skin, blowing through them, as their bodies fight the spirits of the dark, which fly up from the tomb of the damned. Grey imps, two feet in length, with clawed feet and hands, red eyes, lethal pointed teeth and bat wings. Lucifer's low ranking demons, which flap around their prey, screeching, as they attempt to penetrate the burning flames of Notus. They cannot pass through the fires of the gods and so hover outside the circle, waiting, hungry for food and grinding their teeth, sending piercing sounds through the winds into the ears of their prey.

The warlock throws back his ugly head, laughing aloud, as the sound vibrates off the walls, shaking the very core of the crypt, while he mutates into his own self. It is decreed that he must be in the likeness of himself, at the final ravages of death, before he can possess *Grimoire, Book of Shadows*, enabling him to take Charity's essence, placing her shell in the tomb, as he becomes whole again, free to wander the earth, immortal.

'Bloody hell, that's one ugly bugger,' yells Jack, while the others watch in hypnotic fear, as the devil-falcon slowly disappears, re-emerging as the warlock, awakened from his grave, as he sucks the grey ashes of his shell back into himself.

He arises from the ashes of the cursed, the black skeletal, whose soul belongs to the creatures of the underworld. His flesh, rotten and crawling with maggots, his eyes, black hollow holes echoing the emptiness of his soul, and his mouth, a black cavity of vileness, which speaks in the tongues of demons, the Devil's voice. He wears the hooded cloak of the imperishable soul, colourless, lifeless and soulless. In his left hand, he wields the scythe of the oath-breaker, which, with one stroke takes your essence, stealing your mortality for his own, leaving you damned for all time in the shell that becomes your living tomb.

This is a powerful demon and one that requires the blackest of magic to defeat.

Lizzy's words echo through Charity; to fight the beast you must become the beast, and so she calls to the spirits of the underworld, channelling the seven energies of the chakras, opening her mind to the universal unconscious, her all-seeing third-eye, as the doorway to the underworld opens, sending forth the ferocious spirit, Lilith. Imprisoned in the shadows of the underworld, locked in the body of the Druid prophetess by Hecate, the vacuous spirit is, at last, reunited with her Druid descendant, Charity, and the power of two becomes one.

The Inceptor metamorphoses into the female demon, sprouting wings and talons on her feet and hands, while Monty watches, in disengaged abhorrence. Suddenly he sees the power of the beast erupt within her. Is this really his beloved Charity? What has she become? The ugly she-devil he sees before him, this cannot be her, or is it? His heart stops, this is the definitive moment, when he realises that nothing will ever be the same again.

Two demon beasts locked in battle to possess the ancient book of spells, *Grimoire*, as the *Book of Shadows* prophecy is about to be fulfilled.

They fly at each other, Lilith, rapacious, spreading her demon wings, sharpening her talons and licking her demon lips, as the black skeletal comes at her, screaming the vile words of demons, 'Let the plague of Satan's maggots eat at your flesh until the ravages of black death become your living hell.' He prepares to strike her down with his scythe, the two clashing together in mid-air, his coat flapping wildly. Lilith tears into his plague-infested body with her talons, as he grapples to cut her down with his scythe. Savage in her attack, she bites and claws at him, ripping his flesh away, piece by piece, as he struggles to maintain flight, while wielding his scythe,

102

which becomes his enemy, as the weight pulls him down. Lilith violates him, grinding him further and further down, his crumbling body stretched out on top of the tomb, over the cross of his master. She takes the scythe from him, raising it high into the air. He looks up, his hollow eyes fixed with hers, which are brutal in their coldness, as she wields the oath-breaker's blade down upon him, slicing through him, severing what's left of his wretched body in two, as the walls of the crypt tremble with the sound of his screams.

She turns, victorious, standing over her prize, while Monty looks away, loathsome in his feelings for this monster before him. She sees it, and for a moment, the beast's heart melts and a tear trickles down her baleful face, for their saviour, the demon, is still his beloved Charity, but even she cannot deny the ugliness of her other self.

The black storm ceases, as the imps are sucked, screeching with hunger, back into the tomb. The *Book of Shadows* stirs from its death watch, ascending towards Lilith, who takes it, holding it to her chest and merging the two, the angel and the beast, as Charity returns and the prophecy is fulfilled.

'Welcome, dual-spirit, we are yours to command,' says Eurius, bowing, as the others follow suit, while Zephyrus quenches the fires with one sweep of his right hand, before the earth swallows them up and the sacred circle dissipates, leaving the RING stood over the warlock's perished ashes, as Charity becomes the guardian of *Grimoire, Book of Shadows*.

The atmosphere is melancholic, as the RING realise, for the first time, that Charity is leaving them. She is becoming something else, something beyond their mortality, more spirit than human. They fear for her and for themselves, but worst still, they fear for humanity.

Today, evil touched them. It entered their souls and took their innocence, giving them a glimpse of the darkness that sleeps within them all, waiting for the kiss of eternal damnation to awaken it. The beast is within her, two entities at war, but only one will win... Angel or demon?

She feels their fear and sees the torture in Monty's eyes, but she cannot help him or them, for they are right, she is beyond human form now and destiny will decide which world will take her.

'What happens now, Spud?' asks Monty, clutching her hand in his, desperately trying to erase the picture of the beast, Lilith, that is now part of her, hoping against hope that she will never show herself to him.

She holds onto him, his body trembling against hers, as she whispers softly, 'I will always be your angel, remember that, my love, when the darkness comes.'

Silently they cry, knowing that time is against them, and that their dreams of a long life together are just that, a dream.

'Christ, it's moving,' yells Jack, as the ashes of the warlock wake from the dead, forming a grotesque gargoyle, which disappears up the stairs.

'My God, what was that?' asks Sam, almost crushing the life from Leo, as she clings onto him, shaking.

'He is no longer the guardian of the book and so his pact with the Devil is broken and his punishment for failure is finite,' replies Charity.

As they leave, their eyes follow the hideous gargoyle etched into the arch of the vestibule for ever...

12

The Emulating Soul

'Are you all right, my darlings?' shouts Lizzy, breathlessly, running towards them, as they forget their troubles for a moment, laughing hysterically at this roly-poly figure charging towards them, red-faced, perspiring profusely and totally exhausted.

'We are fine, Lizzy.'

'Did yah get the book, my darling?'

'Yes, you did well, Lizzy, very well.'

She smiles, pleased that she has completed her task and that her family is safe, but she sees Charity's face and knows that she knows that one day, soon, she must tell her everything. Charity cannot see Lizzy's secret, because she is trapped in the past, her guilt blocking the truth, and until she releases it, the future cannot be seen.

'Do you possess the power of two now?' asks Leo, as they make their way through the village, towards...

'Where are we going?' asks Robyn.

'So many questions,' quips Charity. 'Yes, I now possess Lilith's spirit within me and the power of two is almost complete, but I still need her soul, only then will I become this all-powerful supernatural being that can stop the Antichrist.

'But she is ugly,' cries Sam. 'Tell me you are not going to end up looking like that?'

'I don't know, Sam,' she replies, squeezing Monty's hand. 'I feel different, yet I am the same. I see both worlds, dark and light, and it is a cross that no one should bear,' she says, touching her necklace of human spirits, comforted by the thought that she has an army of souls to call upon when the time comes.

'You still haven't told us where we are going,' says Robyn, impatient as ever.

'To Mrs Simpson, Jack's new found friend,' she replies, holding the book close to her, knowing that it will be the key to both their futures.

'But I have just come from there,' says Jack, puzzled at why Charity wants to see her when he already has.

'I know, Jack, but she is not what she seems. Tell me what you found out.'

'She is pretty old and repeats herself a lot, but you were right about the village having secrets.'

'What secrets?' asks Sam.

'You are always interrupting before anybody can finish,' digs Robyn, as the two glare at each. Charity smiles to herself, thinking how much she loves her family and how she will miss them when...

She pulls herself back from the darkness. 'You were saying, Jack?'

'It appears that there was a witch craze in the village when ... sorry about this, Monty, some of your ancestors and others in the village were burnt at the stake by the church, one of these witches being a distant relative of Mrs Simpson.'

'Does that make her a witch then?' interrupts Sam again.

'Shush,' growls Robyn.

'She is more powerful than that, she is a pellar,' replies Charity.

'What is that?' asks Lizzy, breathlessly, trying desperately

106

to keep up, having never done so much walking in her life.

'It is an ancient name given to those known as folk witches, powerful witches or warlocks who have the magic to break spells and curses set by others. They can turn a spell or curse against those who cast it. People would go to a pellar when they wanted to break a hex or curse against them, but they always had to offer something in return.' She stops.

'What? What did they have to offer?' asks Robyn, while Sam smirks, pleased that she is being the impatient one this time.

'Themselves, they had to offer their souls before death, which the pellar would keep trapped in a talisman around her neck.'

'What happened when they eventually died?' asks Monty, sensing that somewhere in this tale his ancestors were going to crop up again.

'Their bodies would pass to the pellar, who would keep them with their souls, trapped inside her talisman, giving her immortality. The more souls she had the longer she would live, making her a very dark and dangerous creature, for without the souls of those who sought her help she would die.'

'So how old is Mrs Simpson?' asks Jack, feeling relieved that he managed to leave her house intact.

'Older than humankind, but she is running out of time.'

'What do you mean?' asks Leo, gulping nervously, as they reach their destination and are standing outside Mrs Simpson's house.

'She has no more souls left in her talisman and so is dying, which makes her very dangerous. She needs another soul...'

They look at each other, feeling that shiver of fear

running through them, as Charity rings the doorbell, and the door opens by itself...

'Come in, my dear, I have been expecting you... Ah, Grimoire, so the prophesy has been fulfilled, but you need my services now, my dear,' she says.

They enter a dark, dust-filled room, where light is kept to a minimum by black velvet curtains, permanently drawn, hiding the true face of the old witch who greets them. It is as if time has stood still, everything in the room belongs to another century, the sixteenth, the time of Nostradamus, whose essence lives on in the room.

'Jesus, no wonder you sent Jack instead of Lizzy, this is one creepy place and that is one seriously ugly old hag,' whispers Sam, while covering her mouth at the pervasive smell seeping from her.

Mrs Simpson gives Sam the evil eye, as she quickly hides behind Leo, who steps back a few paces, while Lizzy recognizes the smell; it is the same as the vicar, only far more pungent.

'We meet again, Jack, and so soon,' she sneers, as he steps back, wondering why he did not see her like this before when her creepy looking housekeeper let in him. This is not the Mrs Simpson he has known for years, who cycles around the village, a harmless old woman, befriending everyone with her eccentric, but endearing ways. This is not the room he was standing in earlier today, when the sunlight filtered through the old-fashioned flowery curtains onto the tired old furniture, which looked more like bits and pieces bought from the local charity shop than this dark place. She is not the Mrs Simpson who greeted him so warmly offering tea and scones.

This old woman is ugly. Her teeth are rotten and her face is so old that her skin is falling away, eaten by the ravages of time and her wrinkles are so deep that sores are festering in them. Thin, straggly pieces of grey flea-infested hair hang from her balding head, which sits upon a withered, scraggy old body that is hidden underneath a filthy moth-eaten black velvet coat, which is too big for her, as it trails along the floor. A coat worn by a much taller, majestic woman, not the frail, emaciated one sitting before them.

'So you destroyed the warlock, but the curse still lives and you need my magic to take it away, my dear.'

'You see it don't you?'

'It is within you, eating at your soul and soon it will devour you unless I release you from it. But wait, I see another ... ah but I cannot help you with that one, it was cast by a much higher being than I.'

'What other...?' asks Monty.

'It is OK, honey, we are only interested in the curse I swallowed.'

'You swallowed a curse!'

'It is not as bad as it sounds...'

'Enough of this, I grow tired of conversation,' yells Mrs Simpson, stroking her talisman. 'What can you offer me for my help, my dear?'

'I can give you back your youth without ever having to seek another soul.'

Her grey eyes light up, to have immortality without the need of fresh souls would indeed be a gift she would desire, but how can this be?

'You seek to trick me, Charity, for if there was a way that I could live without fresh souls, then I would have found it.'

'I possess the book now and so can see a way to help us both. I know what happened. I saw it. You were there when the witch craze took place. It was not your ancestors burnt at the stake, but you... You know who cast the spell against she who is last – me. Help me to vanquish this evil spell and I will help you.'

109

'How can you help me?'

'I can summon the Emulating Soul, but before I do you must release me of the curse and let me see the vision of the mirrors.'

'The soul of mirrors,' she says, her frail body shaking with excitement.

'What is this emulating soul of mirrors thing?' asks Leo, totally mesmerized by the haggard old woman who suddenly comes alive, as she dreams of possessing the Emulating Soul.

'It is a clear soul, without substance,' replies Charity, 'which lets you see into it like a mirror, allowing you one vision of the future, but the vision can only be used to help others, not yourself. If you use it with false intentions, then it swallows you into it, and you become the mirror. Whoever possesses the soul of mirrors possesses the key to life for it has within it centuries of souls, which can be trapped in the pellar's talisman, ensuring youth, beauty and immortality.'

'I would not mind possessing this soul myself, to never grow old sounds good to me,' says Sam, visualising her haughty friends getting old and wrinkly, while she remains young and beautiful. Then she looks at the withered old body of Mrs Simpson and suddenly the prospect does not seem so tempting, for she possesses the gift of immortality, but is not looking particularly young or beautiful right now.

'How come you have lost your looks when you have the power to possess souls in your talisman?' she asks, as Leo and the others recoil in horror.

Mrs Simpson laughs aloud, as the others wait, wondering how she is going to react, but Sam amuses her. No one who has ever looked upon her true self has ever dared to ask her that before.

'Each soul that I trap within my talisman ages as I

draw on its essence, and so I need another and then another, but now I have no more souls and soon my body will be so old that I will wither and die. I cannot seek a person who wishes my gift, they must seek me, and there are no more spells to quell in Grimoire village, so I wait for the ravages of time to take me. But, if I had the Emulating Soul, then I would be young again, with the strength to leave this place. I could go where spells and curses are in abundance and I would be the Sovereign Pellar again.'

She feels energised at the thought of feeling the desire and the passion of youth once more, and for a brief moment, she appears young and vibrant. They watch the old hag come alive as the blood of hope runs through her veins.

'What if I give you what you want? How can I trust you to keep your bargain once I vanquish your spell?'

'I have no battle with you, pellar, and wish only to complete my quest. Tell me who placed the curse tablet upon me?'

'Capet Holmes, who was born in 1503 and "died" aged sixty-three in 1566, the same time and age as Nostradamus, whose paths crossed in Montepellier when they were both eighteen and studying medicine. It was then that Capet saw into the future, but unlike Nostradamus his visions showed him being ruler in a kingdom of slaves, so he made a pact with Satan. In return for immortality he would have to destroy the last descendant – you – so that the Antichrist could finally rule. His prize was to be his general. He is the devil's soldier, who sleeps in his grave, waiting to be awoken, and claim his immortality. He gave his soul when the curse tablet was cast in his blood, which now runs through your veins.'

'I think I saw a portrait of him in the hallway, one nasty dark looking son of a bitch,' says Sam, shivering at the thought of his evil eyes looking down upon them.

'Capet Holmes? That name sounds familiar,' says Monty. 'He was deleted from the family tree. It is said that he was an evil man who practised Satanism.'

'Capet, isn't that the name Nostradamus uses in his predictions when referring to any ruler or reigning king?' says Leo

'You are right, Leo, remember, there are no coincidences...' replies Charity. 'Everyone's destiny is decided before life begins and Capet is the one who saw and didn't turn away. He wanted the power that the future could offer and so chose the dark side in order to attain it.'

A raw chill of uneasiness passes over them when they hear the words: 'There are no coincidences...'

'So you are saying that he did not just draw blood from his wrist, but his whole body?' asks Charity.

'Correct, my dear, and that is why his *defixiones* has survived the centuries of time, as he lives within the tablet, which is now within you, waiting for resurrection.'

'How is it that you survived the witch craze when the others did not?' asks Robyn.

'I am the Sovereign Pellar, my body may be burnt, but my souls live on, regenerating, but now...'

'We are back to my offer, pellar, rid my body of Capet's curse and I will summon the Emulating Soul through the *Book of Shadows* and you shall be reborn again.'

They watch and wait, while the pellar looks into the only mirror she possesses since the disease of time took her beauty. She gazes into the cracked mirror, broken in a fit of rage one hundred years ago when the reflection staring back at her was no longer the vision of eternal beauty this vain witch was used to seeing. Since that day, all mirrors were banned from the house, light replaced by darkness, as bitterness became her only companion. She has the power to shape-shift into

112

eccentric Mrs Simpson, and change the world in which she lives, but even this grows less and less as her body disintegrates. Soon she will lose all the power of the pellar, which, if she helps Charity, will use up the last drop of her magic, sending her into the abyss of eternal darkness.

She has no choice. Charity is her last chance and so she grabs it willingly.

'Very well, my dear, I will take your curse tablet, but I cannot turn it on Capet, for his magic is more powerful than mine and I am weak where he is still strong.'

'Where will you send it and what about Capet?' Charity asks.

'I will send it to the crypt, burying it in the tomb of damned souls, where he cannot escape unless it is opened by decree of his new master, the Antichrist. So you must destroy the Antichrist before he awakens Capet and the curse from the tomb.'

'I can live with that, sealed in the crypt, buried in the pit of damned souls, a fitting place for such an evil man.'

'Then let it be, my dear, but remember, once I take the curse from within thee I have only thirty minutes of mortal time before I am no more.'

She lifts herself from the chair, standing upright, as she grows taller, thinner and more youthful, filling out her black velvet coat, which is now sumptuous, as the old hag becomes a pale beauty with porcelain skin and dark, hypnotic eyes that transfix you with their stare. Her hair is black and lustrous, as it tumbles down her back, trailing onto the floor. She is the Queen of Witches, the Sovereign Pellar in all her glory, but this magic has cost her dearly and if Charity cannot fulfil her promise, then this will be the last time she will feel the magic of the pellar within her.

She indicates to the RING to step back, drawing Charity

into the centre of the room, which is no longer dark, but filtered with rays of light that beam down upon her. She looks down to see that she is standing upon a pentagram, a five-pointed star, encased in a circle, which dates back to the twelfth century and is the most important symbol used in witchcraft. There are many uses for the pentagram, but today the pellar will use it to draw out Capet's curse and send it to the crypt.

She takes a black handled athame from inside her coat and points it towards the centre of the pentagram, while speaking in the tongue of the *defixione*, as she awakens Capet's curse tablet.

> *'Capet, I call thee out,*
> *thy curse is blocked,*
> *thy curse is confined,*
> *thy soul is bound where thee can do no harm.*
> ♀
> *Thy body will stew in thine own juices.'*

They wait, but nothing happens, as Charity looks to Monty, who feels powerless, while the others look around, nervously expecting the unexpected, when suddenly they feel it...

The room shakes, as the pellar feels the powerful witch's black magic pulsating through her body, bringing the athame alive with the flames of the *defixione*. The athame shakes violently, bringing forth flashes of fire, which burst out from the tip of its sharp blade, dividing into five flames, igniting each point of the star, imprisoning Charity. The heat is unbearable, as the pentagram is aflame with the fires of the *defixione*. The pellar continues to cast her spell; over and over again she repeats it, while controlling the flames with the athame, until Charity can feel her body being elevated into the air, as the athame guides

114

the flames underneath her, forming a bed of fire, cocooning her within their flames.

The RING can do nothing, as they watch her floating in the air within the pentagram. Suddenly she arches her back causing her arms and legs to dangle, as her head falls back and her mouth opens wide. She screams, the most terrifying of screams, as they see the curse tablet pouring out of her mouth, hundreds and hundreds of pieces of black lead joining together in mid-air, forming Capet's black curse tablet, *defixione*, his spell cast in blood for all to see.

It hovers in mid-air, next to Charity, gripped in the fires of the pentagram, while the pellar raises the athame, pointing it at the tablet, encasing it in the flames that carry it out of the pentagram, through the air, down into the crypt and finally, the coffin, buried with the souls of the damned.

The flames go out and the athame falls from the pellar's hand, as she collapses back into her chair, while Charity descends to the ground, her body lying in the centre of the pentagram.

Monty and the others rush to her, as she slowly comes round and they make their way over to the pellar, who is semi-conscious, and they see her withered body disintegrating before them.

'Hurry, Charity, I haven't much time,' she implores, her voice weak and afraid, as she feels the life force draining from her.

'Quick, the book, Robyn,' Charity shouts, 'we must use the pentagram, it is very powerful and will protect us from Lucifer's demons, which grow angry at Capet's entombment.'

Robyn hands the book to Charity, who stands in the centre of the pentagram.

'The five points must be sealed and the soul catcher

ready. Leo, I appoint you the soul catcher, and the rest, my watchtowers, guardians of the five points.'

'What is the soul catcher?' he asks, suddenly feeling very nervous, as the RING seal the five points of the pentagram, leaving him outside.

'The soul catcher is the most important person in the ritual.'

'You mean no one else is stupid enough to do it.'

Charity senses his anxiety, but knows that she has chosen the right man.

'Once I summon the Emulating Soul it must pass through Mrs Simpson's body if she is to trap it in her talisman, and I need you to catch it for me.'

'Why?'

'Because she is too weak and the soul does not want to be trapped, but I made her a promise and I must keep it, so you must catch it and place it on her talisman, and we will have only once chance to do it.'

Robyn looks at Charity, shocked that she would condemn another soul to such a fate. 'But this soul has done you no harm and you will ask a vision of it only to betray it.'

She knows what Robyn says is right, but she has no choice. She needed the Pellar's magic to rid her of the curse so that she can continue her fight against the Antichrist, but she also needs to see the vision that will help her to find him. The angel inside her wants to protect her world, but the demon spirit that is now her other self knows that sometimes dark deeds are required to fight dark enemies, and so today a sacrifice must be made in order that a greater evil can be stopped.

They look at each other, and, for a moment, Robyn sees and understands, but what if she was in Charity's shoes? Could she be as cruel? This is not Charity. She has changed, become darker; the Inceptor no longer

116

moves amongst angels, but also demons. Which side will take her...?

Charity opens the *Book of Shadows*, while looking to the RING, before casting the spell that will evoke the Emulating Soul.

> *'I am she who commands Grimoire,*
> *I seek the key to the universal doorway of the souls,*
> *Open thy door and let me in.*
> ♀
> *Let the mirrors of light reflect thy vision.'*

The room is still, as they feel the floor quake beneath them. 'Look at the star,' shouts Sam, as they look down to see the five points of the pentagram beneath their feet burning into the floor, cementing their bodies like human poles, which glow. They feel the power of spectral light racing through them, emitting five beams of pure energy that form an impenetrable outer ring around Charity, who waits in the centre for the soul of mirrors.

She feels the touch of elucidatory energy entering her body, rippling through her as the RING watch, unable to move, while her skin ripples, flowing as if in a pond, a clear pond, where if you look closely you can see your reflection. Her whole body moves, forming ripple upon ripple until they see it...

A large clear bubble grows out of her head, getting bigger and bigger until it is floating high above her, attached by an umbilical cord.

'You seek the clarity of the mirrors?' it asks, but they can see nothing. It has no substance, it speaks, but where does the voice come from? The Emulating Soul is a clear, colourless liquid of energy, which, at the hundredth blink of any eye, if you are quick you can see the centuries of souls trapped inside.

117

'I am the Inceptor, the chosen one, and seek the vision of my soul.'

'The three, you seek to join the three? The body, soul and spirit, but what if I grant you your vision? What will you do with your soul?'

'I will have the power of two, dark and light within me, which I must use to stop the coming of the third Antichrist, the King of Terror who waits to walk amongst us.'

'The vision you seek will make you all-powerful, the most supreme supernatural being that has ever walked this earth, but if you fall from the path of light, then I will come for you. Do you still seek the vision of your soul?'

'I do.'

The bubble bursts, as the RING feel a sticky colourless substance cover them. It smells of death, as it leaves behind hundreds of tiny mirrors, joined together with a rope, made out of human skin, which grows from the umbilical cord attached to Charity's head. The mirrors each reflect a vision held within the Emulating Soul.

'Look one of them is getting bigger,' shouts Robyn.

'I see it,' says Monty, as they watch this tiny piece of glass transform into a gigantic three-dimensional mirror, which blinds them as they see their reflection glaring back at them, five beams of pure light that glow all around the room, bouncing off the mirror.

It moves towards Charity who sees her reflection, but within her reflection she sees another, flashing in and out. It is her, her other self, but she is not fair and pretty, but dark and ugly, the beast that lives within the angel. She turns away, for the vision is painful, as truth reflects back, and she sees the ugliness of what she has become. Their own light blinds Monty and the others, but Leo sees and his heart sinks.

'I ask again, do you still seek the vision of your soul?' The voice is deeper and more powerful, but within it is wisdom.

Charity forces herself to look into the mirror. She hates what she sees, but knows she must go on.

'I do, I must.'

'Then let it be, but know this, when the body connects with the spirit and they call to the soul, which makes them one, you cannot go back; when the three become one, you cannot go back...'

Those chilling words cut into her, a deadly dagger that strikes right through her, into the core of her very being, as she prepares to look for her soul... She sees a child, but it is not a child. It has the body of an old woman. The child is asleep, but it is in pain, the pain of old age. It is dying, but it clings on, waiting, waiting for Charity.

'Do you see the child, Charity?' the mirror asks.

'Yes, I see her, she is in pain, so much pain, but she will not let go. Who is she? What is she to me?' she replies with tears in her eyes, tears for the child who is not a child.

'She is the withered child who holds your soul within hers. Find the child and you find your soul.'

'But where do I look?'

'She is where the healing angels watch over her. Look for the castle of the angels.'

The vision disappears along with the mirror, which returns to the Emulating Soul who Charity must now betray...

'Forgive me, but I have no choice.' she whispers, looking into the essence of the soul, which, for a brief moment, appears to shed tears, as she cuts the umbilical cord with the athame, releasing it. Its screams reverberate through her, terrifying screams, which will remain inside her, a living curse of what she has done, as the bubble floats out of the pentagram with its cord dangling.

'Get the cord, Leo, quickly before it disappears,' she shouts, as Leo rushes towards the bubble, which is still screaming. He leaps into the air, grabbing the cord and pulling it towards him. He looks into it. Although it is clear, he can see pain, awful, fearful pain, as the souls within this invisible entity cry out: 'Release us, please release us'.

'Do not listen to them, Leo, close your ears. You must place the bubble onto the talisman, giving life to Mrs Simpson, returning her to the Sovereign Pellar, hurry, Leo, do it now,' she yells, as Leo instinctively does what she asks, but inside he knows there will be a price to pay for the betrayal of this majestic soul.

The talisman becomes a luminous burning flame, glowing brighter and brighter, becoming so hot that it melts into the lifeless body of Mrs Simpson. It burns a hole so vast that it sucks her back into it, leaving behind an empty chair upon which sits a solitary golden disk. As Leo looks closer, he sees the figure of a beautiful dark witch engraved upon it.

'Where has she gone?' he asks, picking up the disk.

'She is reborn in the talisman. Give it to me, Leo,' says Charity, as he throws it to her and she places it in the centre of the five-pointed star, where she leaves it, as she and the RING step back from the pentagram.

The talisman bursts into flames, a glorious multitude of red, blue and yellows fusing together, the flames of eternal life, as they rise higher and higher until they reach the ceiling. The hypnotic flames mesmerize the RING, burning so intensely that they can feel their skin begin to sizzle, when out of the flames she comes...

Mrs Simpson, reborn in all her glory, is a beautiful dark-haired vision with her black velvet coat dripping with red jewels, matching the jewel-encrusted black-handled athame in her left hand, as she walks towards Charity with the regal stance of a queen, the Queen of Witches, the Sovereign Pellar.

'You kept your promise, Charity and I thank you, but I know it cost you a piece of your soul. Betrayal is the darkest of sins and I am afraid your journey into the abode of evil has just begun.' She takes the athame and places it in Charity's hand. 'The Devil's magic must be fought with the Devil's tools. Use it wisely, Inceptor of the angels and goddess of demons.'

Charity takes the knife, but as they leave, she looks back for one last glance, to see old Mrs Simpson sitting in her rocking chair stroking her talisman and smiling...

13

The Demon Shadow

The mood is sombre as they make their way back to Holmes House.

'It wasn't right what you did to those souls, Spud, the old Charity would never have done that; you are not the same, you are not my Spud any more,' whispers Monty, his voice choking, while clutching her hand tightly in his.

'I know, honey,' she replies, her eyes welling up as she pulls him closer, clinging onto him, desperately trying to hold onto who she is. 'I cannot afford to be like her, not this time.'

'Why?' he asks, as Robyn and Sam listen, silently, looking for that glimmer of remorse in her voice to reassure them that she is still their mentor, their angel of light, but Lizzy knows different, she understands, she carries the secret of Charity inside her.

'The other battles where just preludes. The beginning of the beginning of the end...' She stops in the middle of the street, turning to face them, looking into their bewildered faces. 'Good does not always win because it is right ... sometimes the demons win, but that does not mean that we should not fight.'

As they walk up the hill towards the house they remember the words of the Emulating Soul: 'You cannot go back, Charity'. It is then that it hits them; there is no way

122

back from the path that she walks, it only goes one way...

'Will you be in for supper, Mr Holmes, and who will be cooking?' asks Kathy, glaring at Lizzy, who is too tired to care, as they wearily head for the drawing room.

'Yes and whatever you prepare will be most welcome,' he replies looking at Lizzy, who can barely breathe let alone cook a meal for seven tired and hungry souls.

Kathy waltzes off, feeling very pleased that he favours her cooking over Lizzy's, little realising that he does not care what he eats, his appetite has gone, along with his spirit, as he sits silently by Charity, while Jack plays butler with the drinks, downing two large Scotches himself, without blinking.

It seems an age before anyone dares speak, but eventually curiosity gets the better of Robyn. 'What did you see in the mirror?'

Charity touches her necklace, while clutching the pellar's athame in her hand, clinging onto her tools of war, comforted by them, as she feels herself sinking into the abyss of her own insanity.

'I saw a child, a withered child, who is dying in terrible pain, but she is clinging on, waiting for me.'

'Why?' asks Sam, who, like Robyn, is too nosy to stay down for long.

'She holds the key to my other soul, which Hecate took from Lilith, imprisoning it within the heart of the triple goddess, before banishing her into the shadows of the underworld.

'If the triple goddess has your soul then what has this child to do with it?'

'I do not know, Sam, but unless I can unite the three then all is lost.'

'Where is this withered child?' asks Monty, not sure that he wants his wife to become this all-powerful supernatural being, but afraid for the world if she does not. Those dark nagging voices get louder inside his head, as his fears grow stronger; what will become of them all? What will become of Charity and him? His mind wanders back to the church where the so-called vicar married them, only the memory is no longer joyous, but dark and bitter, as he sees the smile on the vicar's face, a smile he once thought was saintly, but now he knows different. He did not bless their marriage, but cursed it, and there is no way back from that.

'She is where the healing angels watch over her. We need to look for the castle of angels,' she replies, rubbing her hands along the *Book of Shadows*, made from living souls. The souls of angels and demons, the essence of good and evil spirits are trapped by the witch's dark magic inside each page of this ancient book of spells. It can summon spirits and demons from both sides of the spirit world, giving whoever commands it undisputed power.

They watch the book. The cover changes colour constantly, from black to blue to red, then green, yellow, and back to black, always the same five colours, whenever Charity touches it.

'The book keeps changing colour whenever you touch it,' says Jack, moving closer, transfixed by it.

Charity gives that knowing little grin of hers when she is about to impart another ancient legendary tale.

'There have been many so-called books of spells written over the centuries, but the book I hold in my hands is the original *Gremoires*, as it was known then, latterly to become, Grimoire *Book of Shadows*, named after the shadows of the gods who created it through the power of the witch's magic in the time of AD 56–120.

'Legend says that Hecate summoned the gods through the power of black magic. They brought with them

124

captured souls from heaven and hell, which, through the witch's magic, became imprisoned in the written word on the pages of the book. Each spell was written down with the essence of the souls whose spirits bind the pages. The cover was made up of the gods who created it.

'Hecate, the triple goddess of the underworld, who has the power to see into the past, present and future is represented by black. Eurius, Lord of Air is blue; Notus, Lord of Fire, red; Zephyrus, Lord of Water, green; and Boreas, Lord of Earth, yellow. Five gods, five colours, five supernatural powers, all contained in the *Book of Shadows*, but only the one who can make its cover change to the colour of the Gods has the power to command it.'

'No wonder the warlock and the witch wanted it, but how come the witch, I mean Mrs Simpson, did not try to take your essence and the book like the warlock?' asks Robyn.

'Only I can summon the Emulating Soul. Even if she destroyed me and took my essence, her magic would not be able to summon the soul of mirrors. It only comes to those who seek to do good things with its visions.' She holds back the tears ... 'And I betrayed it...'

Monty squeezes her hand, as the others, though sad to see her cry, are secretly pleased that she still can.

'Anyway we digress, back to the withered child and the castle of angels, any ideas anybody?' she asks.

'Why can't you just use your powers and the book now that you are almost this all-powerful supernatural creature?' asks Sam, puzzled that one minute she sees and knows all and can transform herself into supernatural beings, and the next she cannot even find a child.

'It does not work like that, I do not choose what I see, it chooses me, and the visions or voices are as cryptic as Nostradamus's quatrains. I feel like I am in a huge maze where I am slowly trying to find my way out, and along the way I am given signs and clues, but it is up to me how I interpret them.'

'Just like when you use the tarot.'

'Exactly, Robyn, just like that. The tarot is a tool used by the inceptor to unlock the collective unconscious, the imagery and symbols stimulate the all-seeing third-eye, whereby the interpreter can see the vision of the story unfold before them through the cards. But is just that, a tool, which is as good or as bad as the inceptor using them, but when the cards are in the right hands it becomes a very powerful tool...'

'What is the difference between hearing voices and seeing visions, be it through the cards or another divinatory tool?' asks Leo, slowly finding himself becoming more intrigued by this ancient mantic art. Where once he mocked, now he sees that it is not the tool that has the power, but the person who interprets it.

'It is difficult to explain. The voice is an invisible message inside my head, it is like my own voice talking back to me, yet I know it's not me, unlike when you chat away to yourself when trying to clarify things in your own mind. Immediately I know or understand things that I did not before, a bit like a revelation; one minute I am ignorant and the next I seem to know all. It is akin to the most powerful of our basic animal instincts, intuition. As an inceptor, I nourish my intuition, using it constantly, until it becomes my very being. I cannot bring the voices on; they come without invitation, unlike a vision when I actively summon one by channelling my gift through the cards or another divinatory tool. Even they are not always in my control, the flashing visions and the ones that come to me in my psychic dreams. The ones sent by other forces, which can be perilous, when I have no means of escaping them.'

126

'I am still learning to channel my intuition, but it is difficult, I cannot always know if what I am feeling is truth or lie,' says Robyn, the sponge seeking to soak up more knowledge.

Charity laughs that little chuckle of hers, when she sees her niece so desperately wanting to learn. It is a comfort to her to know that one day she will live through ... her mind wanders, but she brings it back, sharply, focusing only on the present.

'As time goes on and your powers grow, combined with your knowledge, you will know which is truth or lie, but remember, you are not spirit but mortal and therefore not infallible, and so sometimes you will be misled, but that is the price all inceptors pay for the privilege of being what we are.'

'So what you are saying is that you heard a voice, an invisible voice inside your head, telling you to seek out Mrs Simpson, who would rid you of Capet's curse in exchange for the Emulating Soul. But first the soul must show you the vision of the withered child, which is the next clue or sign in this maze that you are in.'

'In a way, Leo, I am in control, but then I am not, I just follow the path that has been set for me and it is up to me whether I choose to use or ignore the signs along the way.'

'So what do we do now that you do not appear to have any more signs?' asks Sam.

'I summon one, like I said, sometimes I am in control and other times I am being controlled.'

'The tarot, you will use the cards,' says Robyn excitedly, for she loves it when Charity calls upon the symbols of these ancient tools. They are her most favourite divinatory tool, which, like Charity, she is never without, always carrying some with her, just in case she needs to call upon their wisdom.

'But why not use the book, surely its magic will show you the way?' asks Monty, wondering why she cannot use the most powerful tool that she possesses.

'Not this time, honey, my intuition tells me when it is right to use certain tools and this is not the time to use the book, I just know it.'

'What cards will you use?' asks Robyn.

'The Major Arcana, and if you will prepare the table, Robyn, I will go and get them.'

Charity makes her way to her bedroom, while Robyn and the others prepare the room, but as she walks up the stairs and along the hallway, she feels something touch her. She looks around, but there is nothing there, yet her body is telling her otherwise. She stands there, her feet frozen into the ground, looking around this vast, dark, cold hallway, which suddenly appears even more sinister, as Monty's ancestors seemingly come to life. Their portraits close in on her, their smiles becoming evil sneers, which seem to be jeering at her, taunting her with their whispers...

'Be careful, Charity, what you wish for will be your undoing; the power to see is the instrument of your demise...'

She feels it again ... it grips her shoulder, cutting into her, as she swings round. Her whole body trembles, as she struggles to breathe, but still she sees nothing. Something brushes past her, a shadowy figure ... not human ... it pushes her over the balcony...

She grips on tightly to the banisters, slowly pulling herself back up, as the hallway gets darker, portraits closer and the whispers louder, until, eventually, she makes it back to the bedroom, but just as she closes the door, she feels it again...

It brushes into her, sending her into a breathless panic. She feels her chest tightening and her body numbing, while her legs give way and she crumbles to the floor. She cannot move, her body frozen with fear, as she sees it floating in front of her. A dark creature. The shadow of a demon, its eyes flashing, red penetrating eyes that look into her soul, touching her with its evil. Slowly it moves in and around her, as she desperately tries to summon the beast within her to fight it, but her powers are useless.

Where are her guardian angels, Ma and Pa? Where are her gods? Where is her power of the shape-shifter? Why is she unable to summon them? Why is she so alone, so helpless, when she is supposed to be so powerful?

It is upon her. She cannot breathe, her body fixed against the door, her hands and feet immobile as it enters her, consuming her with its evil thoughts, as she sees herself wandering in the darkness, alone, afraid and powerless. She sees the gate, the gate of penitent souls, only this time she is on the other side looking back, back at what she has lost.

She feels pain, torturous, unforgiving pain, spreading through her body like a plague, devouring her, as she wanders in the darkness, trying to find her way back. Through wretched souls, crying and screaming, clawing at her body, dragging her further and further down into the pit of the underworld, where she sees the fires of eternal damnation, waiting for her. The flames get closer and closer, she hears the voice of Annie calling to her, 'Go back, Charity, please go back'. But she cannot, there is no one to help her, she is alone, as the flames draw closer and closer...

Suddenly the vision disappears and she feels herself returning, as it leaves her. The demon shadow pours out of her body, floating past her and out of the window, but as it vanishes, she hears the words:

'When the three become one you cannot go back, Charity...'

She rushes to the bathroom, pouring water over her face, as she looks into the mirror and sees the reflection of a damned woman staring back at her. There is a burning pain in her left shoulder. As she looks down she sees the sign of the Antichrist ‡ branded into her. Her heart sinks. She has been marked...

She pulls herself together and collects her cards, her body white and shaking, as she makes her way back to the RING, who see that she is different, but no one dares to ask the question that they all fear the answer to...

14

The Withered Child

Charity shuffles the cards, as she feels the heat of Satan's mark burning into her.

'Are you OK, Spud, you keep touching your shoulder?'

'I am fine, honey, just tired that is all, it has been a long day.'

'Then perhaps you shouldn't do the cards, they take so much out of you,' says Robyn, knowing that something is very wrong, but too afraid to use her gift to see.

'No, we do not have much time, the child is dying and I sense that she must be alive to pass on the soul.'

Everyone is silent, as she shuffles the cards one last time, while closing her eyes to perform the chakras, slowly opening her mind to the universal unconscious, her all-seeing third-eye.

'I am ready.'

She places the pack face down on the table spreading the cards evenly into a fan. She draws out two cards, placing them in the centre, then another just above the two and finally one more above the one, until she has four cards, face down, forming a pyramid. The base represents the past, the middle, the present and the point, the future.

She turns them over.

The past: The Tower and the Three of Pentacles
The Present: The Hanged Man
The Future: The Black Horseman

'What do you see?' asks Robyn, who sees into the cards,
but holds back, waiting for her mentor's interpretation.

'I see the burning tower of shattered dreams, shock
and despair, but out of the flames of disaster I see a
new beginning. The supporting arch of the three pentacles
is the foundation of the castle where the angels watch
over her. The hanged man, who is suspended in time,
waiting to be released to the black horseman of death
who will take her to the place of serenity that is in her
dreams, but only if I come in time.'

'So we are looking for a castle then?' asks Monty.

'Half right, honey. In the thirteenth century, a castle
burnt down along with the king and all his people who
lived in the nearby village. They where stricken by a plague,
one thousand men, women and children were buried *en
masse*. Centuries went by and the earth swallowed them up
into the land, forgotten, as a succession of buildings were
built upon their graves, until finally we come to now, where
the foundations of a hospital sit upon this ancient burial
ground of one thousand unconsecrated souls. Amongst
the souls was a woman who held in her hand a bulla, a
sacred document from the Pope, a prayer, paid for by her
to send her soul into the afterlife.

'The bulla was false. Her family kept the money and
gave her a lie, burying her without cleansing her soul of
her sins, denying her entry into the afterlife. So she cursed
them from the grave, where her soul still lies, waiting;
that they should suffer the perils of the plague from
birth till death.'

'You saw all that in the cards?' asks Leo, amazed at
what four little cards can produce.

132

'The symbols on the cards were merely the tool that unlocked my collective unconscious, once I opened my third-eye through the chakras. It is then that I saw the vision of the plague, which beset the village and its entire people, who were buried side by side, the good and the bad, rich and poor, young and old, some in coffins, others in shrouds, lost in the pit of forgotten souls.'

'But what about the woman and the curse, what connection is she to the child in your vision?' he asks.

'The child carries the curse of the betrayed soul, which has been passed down through the centuries to a chosen few, of which she is the last. The curse will be vanquished with her, at the place where it was cast, the pit of forgotten souls.'

'I get it, the last descendant waits for the last descendant,' shouts Sam.

'Is that right, Spud?'

'Partly, honey, but it is not that simple and I cannot see everything, and so we must find the hospital to complete the puzzle of the child who possesses my soul.'

'The papers in the library – I remember seeing something there about a hospital, perhaps that is the link?' says Leo, excitedly.

'Once again your legal brain is sharper than a razor. Can you find the papers?' asks Charity.

'No problem, leave it to me,' he replies, rushing off to the library with Sam in hot pursuit, and beaming with smug pride at the two of them being central in this latest puzzle in their quest.

'I think we should get ready to go out after dinner,' she says, collecting her cards as Jack, Monty and Lizzy rush off for a quick wash and change of clothes, leaving Robyn behind.

'You did not tell them everything that you saw in the

cards,' she says, looking at Charity, who continues to pack away her cards, avoiding her gaze.

'There was nothing more to tell,' she replies sheepishly, walking away, leaving Robyn standing in the drawing room, rubbing her shoulders, as she feels the sudden chill of doom enter her bones...

'I have found it,' shouts Leo, as they rush into the library, where he and Sam are entrenched in a sea of papers, grinning like the cats that have found the cream.

'It was a private hospital built in 1666 by another one of your ancestors, Monty, a Dr Legan Holmes, who, according to the family history, was a sickly child that became a doctor. However, due to increasing bad health he retired aged forty-one, and became a recluse, living the rest of his life at Holmes House. He spent the last years of his life trying to find a cure for the disease that ravaged his body, for which there seemed to be no medical explanation. He went bankrupt spending all his money on research and building his own hospital, employing eminent doctors and scientists to experiment on people who suffered from unknown and incurable illnesses in a quest to find the answers to his own decaying body. He eventually died in 1676, aged forty-eight, the year the hospital mysteriously burned down.'

'Jesus, Monty, I hate to say it, but your family is one weird lot. Witches, demons and now a mad doctor – what other dark secrets are still lurking underneath the Holmes mask of respectability?' says Jack, shaking his shoulders, trying to brush off that feeling of impending doom that has been constantly following them around since they came back to Holmes House, which he used to love, but now cannot wait to leave.

Monty grins, but he can feel their eyes boring into

him, judging him, and wondering if they really know him at all. 'This is as much a surprise to me as it is to you lot,' he says, glancing over to Charity, who knows that he is innocent. He looks to her for reassurance as their entire lives seem to be crumbling around them.

'Everyone has their secrets and skeletons, Jack,' she says, joking, but underneath, he feels her gift looking right through him. He knows that she knows that he is no innocent either, that his family have their own dark secrets, which he has buried deep in his own soul. He is a good man, but he comes from a bad lot and so he, more than anyone, should know better than to throw the first stone at the only man who has shown him a brother's love.

'I did not mean anything by it. It is just that everything we have uncovered about the Holmes family, so far, seems to have a dark, sinister connection. I...'

'It's OK, Jack, I understand, old buddy, it has been a bit of a revelation to me as well, and I am supposed to be one of them,' says Monty, laughing, but underneath still feeling like he has been punched in the gut.

'Have you noticed something else that is creepy?' says Robyn, eager to share her knowledge.

'What?' asks Sam, annoyed that she may have discovered something they have missed, while Charity smiles quietly to herself, as she too has seen what her niece is about to point out.

'The name Dr Legan Holmes; it is an anagram of angel, and then there is the date when the hospital was built 1666....'

'What is odd about that?' interrupts Sam, feeling decidedly put out that she did not manage to work that one out.

'The three sixes, they are the sign of the Antichrist and, it may be a long shot, but I do not think so: the number one in 1666, I think that stands for one thousand...'

Everyone is still ... except Charity.

'The one thousand years of darkness, *Quatrain 77*, and the one thousand souls, once again there is that insidious feeling that there are no coincidences...' she says, smiling.

'Does that mean Dr Legan, I mean Dr Angel is in league with the Devil?' asks Sam, feeling that creepy chill again.

'The only way to be sure is to find the hospital and the child,' replies Charity, looking at Leo, who has a map.

'It is in the grounds somewhere,' he says.

'No it cannot be, I would know. I know every bit of my land. I have ridden over every piece of it over the years and I have never seen a hospital,' says Monty, grabbing the map from him, angrily.

Everyone scrutinizes the map; there is no hospital. They become increasingly frustrated until Lizzy spots it.

'There it is, my darlings, Angel Church, it has got to be it.'

'Yes, yes, you have done it again, Lizzy,' yells Charity, kissing her on the cheek, as she turns bright purple.

'But that is a derelict building. It has not been a church for years; in fact I cannot remember the last time anybody has been there,' says Monty, inspecting the map again, and wondering why he did not make the connection.

'What do you know about this church?' asks Leo.

'Not much, my parents told me that it was built long before they were born, but were always vague about who built it and why. Everyone that has visited it has said that it felt strange ... but I never remember it being a hospital. I do remember going there as a child. I was out riding one day and came across it; you know secret old places that children find irresistible. I went inside ... it was dark and I could barely see, but there was definitely something there...'

136

'What was it?' asks Robyn, her body frozen with anticipated fear.

'I felt as if I was being watched, yet there was definitely no other human there except me, but I am sure that something brushed past me, whispering. I could not make out what they or it was saying. Anyway it spooked me and I ran out of there like the wind without looking back.'

'That sounds more than spooky to me,' says Robyn.

'Well I think it is time for a second visit, honey,' says Charity, as they all get that squirming feeling in the pit of their stomachs. This old church is not what it seems...

'How much longer before we are there?' moans Lizzy, fed up with walking everywhere, as they follow Leo, map in hand. As they get closer, Monty begins to get that feeling again.

'Here it is,' says Leo, stepping inside.

'Whose idea was it to come here at night?' says Sam, her skin crawling with nervous foreboding.

They stand in the centre of the church, a dark, malevolent building, with the smell of death seeping from its crumbling walls. The ground beneath their feet feels like quicksand, as the stone floor gives way to black earth alive with slimy bugs and maggots, which crunch as they walk over the graves of forgotten souls.

They can feel the building closing in on them, trying to swallow them up, as a bitter cold wind blows through the walls, whispering... 'Release us, please release us'.

'I felt something touch me,' screams Sam, as she turns around to see, nothing...

'I did too,' yells Robyn, who can see something ... but it is too faint. 'Can you see it, Charity,' she says, spinning around the aisle, as the others stand at the foot of the altar, looking up at a cross, which is upside down, the sign of the Antichrist.

Charity can see a figure floating above the pulpit, a small, grey figure; the spirit of a child. She moves towards it, while the RING form a circle, back to back, as they feel themselves being sucked into this evil place, while Robyn follows Charity up the aisle towards the pulpit.

'What is it Charity, what do you see?' asks Robyn.

'I am not sure, it looks like the ghost of a small child, but there is something strange about it,' she says, as the two of them slowly edge their way to the pulpit, while the RING remain frozen with fear at the alter, unable to move. The ghost becomes clearer and the cross bigger, forming a huge dark shadow that towers over them.

'It is an old woman, but in a child's body,' yells Robyn, as they finally come face to face with the withered child.

'I have been waiting so long for you, Charity, so very long,' she says, her body thin and balding, with a wizened narrow face and the skin of an old woman. She looks about eighty years old, yet has the voice and frame of a ten-year-old child.

'Who are you?'

'I am the keeper of your soul, Charity, given to me by Hecate, when the curse of the bulla struck me down in the year of my birth, 1666. The year of the coming of the Antichrist, who moved amongst us in the form of the beast, killing all that was before him, until he found the soul that gave him mortal life.'

'He is amongst us now?' asks Charity, her body shaking with shock.

'He has always been here. He has wandered the earth since 1666, taking whomever he chooses. Twice he ruled, but lost to the power of man, but now he is ready to rise again, and this time they will not be able to stop him.'

138

Charity and the RING cannot believe what they are hearing.

'Napoleon and Hitler, twice he ruled amongst us,' she whispers.

'Your gift is strong, Charity, but you cannot see the third, which hides amongst you, more cunning and powerful than he has ever been. He knows the third will be his rule, but fears the three, body, spirit and soul; the Inceptor, who will become one in the power of two – his equal. You are his nemesis, and he must destroy you, so that he can reveal his true self...'

'But we stopped his coming at Kradlived, we destroyed his children, the Dark Trio, Lucifer lost, we won.'

'There is only one. A malignant force; an evil organism that absorbs all that it touches and Lucifer is its host, the Devil Octopus, the dark creature of the underworld, whose tentacles reach out, corrupting everything that it touches. It cannot die; destroy its tentacle and you kill just one part, replaced by another, spreading its evil seeds again. Napoleon, Hitler, his children; you only stop the tentacles, not the source...'

'But that means we will never win?'

'Evil is the other side of good, the yin and yang, which constantly battle for control, but as long as balance remains, then you win. Keep the balance, Charity. Destroy the third tentacle, the third Antichrist. Stop the prophesied *Quatrain 77*; stop the one thousand years of darkness that will tip the scales of balance over into the side of evil...'

'The cross, Charity, look at the cross,' shouts Monty, as they all look up to see it suspended over them, its shadow preparing to devour them, while the withered child floats above the pulpit, afraid.

'There is not much time, Charity, if you do not take the soul I cannot be released from the disease of progeria.'

139

'I have heard of that, it is a rare medical condition where children are born genetically predisposed to premature ageing. They show all the symptoms of old age, where one year of their life spans eight. The loss of body fat and hair, stiffness of joints, arthritis and hip dislocation, blood pressure, angina, enlarged heart, and eventually, death by heart attack. They literally die of old age, but are still only a child, as they rarely live beyond their tenth year. It is a sad, painful death, which cannot be stopped, as there is no cure.'

'You have the name for it now, but when I was born it was called the curse of bulla, and whoever it marked, had to be marked, so no one would catch it. They burned down my parents' house and sent me to the House of Withered Children, Angel Hospital, where all those who were born with the disease of bulla were sent. There I waited to die, but when my time was due, I was offered life, but at a price.

'Hecate, the triple goddess came to me in a vision and promised the gift of eternal youth in return for becoming, the keeper of your soul, but only when you come to claim it. So I have waited since 1676, the year of my death, for you to come so that I can finally know the peace of eternal youth and not the pain of old age.'

'But why give you the soul, why not give it to me herself?' Charity asks.

'You must take it from the one who bears the mark of bulla, at the place where the one thousand forgotten souls wait to be released; free the souls and you free yourself from the mark of Satan, which will be your own nemesis.'

Charity touches her shoulder, which burns into her skin like the fires of hell, as she looks up at the cross, which is almost upon them.

'When did the hospital become the house of Satan?'

'When I became the last to carry the curse of bulla,

140

the year of my vision when Hecate made me the keeper of your soul and the ghostly watchtower of the grave of forgotten souls. This was the year that darkness fell upon this spot, and the penance of the long wait began.'

The cross is almost upon them...

'Hurry, Charity, please hurry,' screams Sam, crouched to the ground and huddled together with the RING, with the cross about to swallow them up.

Charity looks at the cross and then over to the child, holding the *Book of Shadows* close. What should she do...? If she fights for the RING, then she will lose the child, but if she takes the soul, then she will lose the RING...

'I cannot win,' she yells, as Robyn shouts:

'The necklace, Charity, use the necklace.'

She pulls it from her neck and throws it towards the RING, as they lie on the floor, waiting for the cross to take them.

The disk glows into a ghost light, blinding the surface of the RING with its heavenly light, as the chain of human spirits metamorphoses into human hands, hundreds of hands that cling to the cross, pulling it up, away from the RING, until it is floating high above the aisle. The cross fights to descend, as the hands pull it back, but they are stronger, dragging it out of the church into the night sky, where the ghost light follows, and they see it strike into it, exploding it into oblivion.

The hands and light become one, as the necklace flies back into the church, returning to its master, Charity. A bright light enters the church, lifting the shadow of Satan from it, as the withered child floats towards Charity, arms outstretched, smiling.

'Feel my embrace, Charity,' she says, folding her arms around her. Their bodies touch and Charity feels the power of the gods entering her. She screams, her body

141

shaking uncontrollably, convulsing into violent spasms. The soul of Lilith leaves the child and enters her ... and the power of three becomes one, joining the power of two. She is reborn...

The child floats back to the pulpit, as Charity feels the beast raging through her. She sees it all, the two worlds, heaven and hell. The power of two is within her, beast and angel, held within the vessel of her mortal body. Body, spirit and soul are as one. The prophecy is fulfilled. She is all-powerful, the supreme supernatural being, but the words of the Emulating Soul echo inside her...

'When the three become one, you cannot go back...'

The RING stare in hypnotic bewilderment, as Monty holds back the tears – he has lost her. They have witnessed something beyond human cognizance. She looks the same, but they know she is no longer theirs; she belongs to another world now...

'Look at the child,' shouts Sam.

The ghost of the withered child begins to evolve; old woman replaced by the child, a beautiful blond girl, with the smile of an angel and the body of pure perfection. She dances around the aisle, her body light like air and her laughter full of the joyous mischief of youth, free from the pain of old age.

As she dances, she sees it...

The black horseman rides out of the shadows, towards her, picking her up, as the black stallion rears up, turning on its hind legs, facing Charity. 'Remember, look for the mark of the beast, Charity, whoever bears the mark is the third.'

'Where do I look?'

'Look for the angel who is not an angel, where the beast devoured the flesh of man to become man,' she replies, as the horseman rides off into the night.

The earth sucks the church into the ground, as the

142

walls crumble, while they race to escape the missiles of falling bricks. Within minutes, it disappears, the quicksand of forgotten souls replaced by living grass. Hundreds and hundreds of small balls of light fly up from the earth into the sky, one thousand ghost lights, which shimmer and shine, lighting up the night sky, as they join together forming a night rainbow, which stretches up into the heavens.

15

The Incubus

Charity looks in the mirror, the face is the same, but the woman is not...

'How long will you be, Spud? It is getting late,' shouts Monty from the bedroom, trying to behave as if everything is normal, when inside he is in turmoil. Who is the woman in the bathroom performing her usual nightly ritual? Who will sleep beside him tonight? Will it be his gently loving wife, Charity, or the spirit beast, Lilith? His heart sinks, as he waits.

'Not long, honey, nearly finished,' she replies, her voice normal, but inside she is distraught. She rubs her shoulder, the mark has gone, but the scar remains. If only she could turn back the clock and just be Charity Holmes, Monty's wife, not this being that she has become. Why her, why must she be the one?

'I keep looking at you, Charity Holmes,' she says, staring at her reflection, 'but you cannot help me, no one can help me. Where are you, Ma, Pa and Annie? Why do you not come to me? I need you and you have forsaken me. I am alone, so very alone...'

She wipes away the tears, trying desperately to be what Monty wants her to be, but they both know that they walk the path of destruction ... two silent souls, grieving for each other, neither willing to let the other see their pain.

'Well it has been another hell of a day, Spud,' he says, holding her tight, as she clings to him, afraid of what the night spirits will bring in her dreams.

'Goodnight, honey, sleep well.'

She closes her eyes and darkness falls.

'I cannot get back, help me, please help me...' she screams. She is scratching at the earth, digging her way out to the other side, the other side of the gate, the gate of penitent souls. She is on the wrong side, fighting to escape from the underworld, where all the fallen souls tear at each other, frantically clawing their way out of their own wretchedness. It is hopeless, as they scream and beg for absolution, for a second chance, for peace.

'I am not one of you, I am the Inceptor, I belong on the side of the angels, open the gate, let me out, please, I should be on the other side; you have made a mistake. Tell them, my Lord; I am not one of them...' she cries, as the souls claw at her, screaming their wretched cries. 'Please, someone stop their cries...'

The nightmare continues, down, deeper and deeper she goes, dragged, screaming into the darkness. Something grips her shoulders, pulling her back, carrying her up through the pitiful souls that cling onto her, desperate to escape, only to fall away, as she flies through the darkness, faster than a single breath, until she sees light.

Her body, floating high above the gate, is clasped gently in the claws of a magnificent bird, the peregrine falcon, her Lord, in the form of the beast. She looks down upon the abyss of misery beneath her, as he spreads his spectacular wings, flying through the night skies, taking her back through the chasm of time. Wallowing in his protective embrace, she hears the whisper of the night angels, singing to her, comforting her with their sweet

145

sounds. He stops, suspended in the skies, as she looks down to see... Lizzy...

But, as she looks closer, sees that Lizzy is different. She is young and beautiful with her long, dark, silky hair trailing across the crisp white sheets, as her pale face rests peacefully on a pillow. She is the most beautiful of creatures, a dream woman, who sleeps wistfully in the night, dreaming of love and...

He comes to her, through the shadows of her night dreams; the incubus, a fallen angel, the demon incubus who preys upon vulnerable women, raping them in their sleep, fulfilling their secret carnal desires. He lies upon her, a handsome, virile creature. Everything that she desires in her dreams he is, as she succumbs to his lustful embrace. She is in ecstasy, as the passion of his lovemaking pulsates through her body, elevating her into raptures of exalted pleasure that only a dream lover could give...

He leaves, as he came, disappearing into the shadows while she lies there, her body ravaged by the beast incubus, the angel who is not an angel.

The falcon lifts Charity up again. Through the night skies they fly, as she struggles with the vision of Lizzy. Suddenly they stop. They are in the same place; it is the same room, the same bed, but the woman and time are different. She sees Annie, sleeping, restless, as her dream takes her to another place, a dark place, where the incubus comes again, but this time he is not what she desires, as she wakes, finding him upon her, the demon incubus in all his ugliness. She fights him, her cries of despair raging through the night, but he wins, as he takes her.

Another woman rushes in, it is Lizzy, distraught at what she sees. He turns, laughing at her, as he takes Annie again and again, while she watches, helpless. Annie's screams turn to emptiness, as he disappears into the shadows, leaving them, desolate in their wretchedness.

146

Charity's heart is broken, as the vision disappears and the falcon carries her off into the night skies, showing her vision after vision. One thousand souls, buried in a pit of despair. The withered child, born into hell and wrenched from the arms of her mother, who falls to her knees, killed by the flames of her burning home, as her child is carried to her prison by Dr Legan, a diseased, ravaged, condemned man.

Angel Hospital is awash with blood. One thousand screaming men, women and children, slaughtered in their beds, as the beast rages amongst them. The flesh of man ... to become man.

She sees Dr Legan, standing, wretched and alone, as the hospital burns to the ground, leaving nothing but, black ash, as the beast enters him...

The angel who is not an angel has become man ... the third man...

The seed of the third tentacle has spread its evil...

The third Antichrist is here...

16

The Secret

Lizzy can sense Charity's eyes burning into her, as she lays the table for breakfast, while Robyn is busy checking her notes, going over everything that has happened looking for the next sign or clue in the TIE.

'What is it, my darling, why do you keep staring at me?' she asks, worried that she has seen her secret, now that she has the power of two within her.

'I need to speak you alone, Lizzy.'

'Not now, my darling, I am busy,' she replies, avoiding her gaze.

'No, this cannot wait,' she snaps, her voice trembling.

Everyone stops, looking at her, shocked, as Lizzy drops Jack's breakfast.

'What is it, Spud, what is wrong?' asks Monty, afraid. Her voice is different, colder, sharper, it is not hers, but the other one, Lilith.

'Nothing, honey, everything is fine, it is just that we have so much to do and so little time and I just need to speak to Lizzy before I...'

'It is OK, Monty, I know what Charity wants, eat up my darlings, we will not be long.' she replies, following Charity into the library, as the others sit, silently eating.

'You know, my darling, you saw,' she says, shaking

'How could you, Lizzy, why, why did it happen?'

148

'I am sorry, my darling, I did not wish for it to happen, I did it to protect you.'

'I do not want to be protected, I want the truth, tell me the truth.'

'I desperately wanted a child, even though I had no man, but I carried the curse.'

'What curse?'

'All the woman in our family are barren, bereft of the ability to bear children; my beloved sister, Mary, my mother and her mother and all the mothers before her, all sterile...'

'Like me, I am bereft of child too...' Charity says, her body trembling with rage and shock.

'No, you are special, you were not conceived like the others. Mary escaped the curse of the demon lover; you are the last my darling, and with you the curse dies.'

'But what about Robyn? She was conceived after me, through a dream, like Annie, so I cannot be the last.'

'Robyn is not of the beast, Annie saved her.'

'What do you mean?'

'Annie saw who he was, when I could not. I was weak, but she was stronger. She fought and would not let him have her, not like me, when I let him have Annie.'

'How do you mean, let him have Annie?'

'In a moment of weakness, when I dreamed of a lover, I wished for him to come, and when he did, I let him into me willingly, and so he sowed his seed of evil, while I was blinded by lust and desire. I gave life to his beast, Annie. When I awoke, I was despairing in my shame, praying to my Lord to forgive me my sin of lust, and to protect my Annie, who I felt inside me the moment his seed entered.

'She grew into a beautiful child and woman, gentle and loving, and so I thought my Lord had saved her. I gave myself to him, devoting my life to prayer and my family,

149

but I was wrong, he punished me by punishing her. When she dreamed of her lover, she awoke and saw the beast. Fighting him, she did not give herself willingly, and so Robyn was not his, but in doing so, she sealed her fate.'

'What fate?'

'When she died, the beast took her, imprisoned her deep in the underworld, where he tortures her with visions of Robyn, her beautiful daughter that she can never hold in her arms. She cannot come to you, my darling, he holds her to him, but she waits, waits for you to come and save her. Please, you must help my beautiful Annie.'

Lizzy crumbles to the floor, the burden of her secret finally released, as Charity holds her in her arms, rocking her back and forth like a baby, as she cries uncontrollably, pleading for forgiveness.

'I could not tell you, my darling, I dared not tell you. I cannot tell Robyn, how can I tell her that her mother is really my ... daughter, and that her father, like Annie's, is the demon incubus, the Devil lover, sent to seduce us in our dreams to produce his seed?'

'Please do not cry, Lizzy, it will be OK, Annie will be OK, I will find her, I promise I will find her,' she says, crying, as the two of them cling onto each other, desperately. They hold each other tightly, until the tears run dry and there is no more crying left in them, as they slowly pull themselves together, making their way to the couch.

'I still do not understand,' Charity says, wiping her face, while Lizzy pictures the last time she saw Annie, laughing, as she played with Robyn in the garden.

'What is that, my darling? There will be no more secrets between us.'

'Where does Robyn get her gift from, if Annie is not my sister?'

'My Lord, he gave her the gift when Annie fought

150

back. He saved her, he answered my prayer through Robyn. She is like you, my darling, she is of the angels; she is the next inceptor.'

'But, if what you say is true, I am different from Robyn, my father is not of the beast incubus, and my mother is not of the angels, but of the underworld,' she says, trembling.

'You are the chosen one, my darling, whoever your parents be. My Lord has decreed that you have the gift of the two worlds, dark and light. You were conceived by divine decree...'

The room is still, as Lizzy's words dissipate into the air, while they ruminate the dark secrets of their past. Are all the secrets out? Is this the end of Charity's search for the lineage of her past? Something is missing. She looks at Lizzy, a broken woman, who has lived a lie for over forty years, but sees that there are no more secrets within her.

Her gift of sight fails her, something darker and more powerful than she is blinding her to the truth ... but she will find it out, whatever it is.

'What are you two up to? You have been gone a long time, what secrets are you keeping from us?' jokes Robyn, as Lizzy and Charity look at each other.

Who is going to tell her?

Lizzy knows it must be her. She sits her down, telling her the dark secrets of her past, and who her father really is.

'I do not believe you,' she screams, pacing the room, hysterical with grief, at discovering that her mother was violated by a dream demon, and that her father is this beast, who is also the father of her mother.

'Please, you must understand, Robyn, it was not my fault.'

'Not your fault,' she yells, as everyone comes running into the room, her screams resonating through the house.

151

'What is going on?' asks Monty, rushing towards Robyn.

'Do not touch me, leave me alone,' she screams, pushing him away. Everyone stands in mortified horror, as she rants and rages at Lizzy, who cowers in the corner, her body collapsed on the floor, crying uncontrollably, begging for her forgiveness.

'What has happened?' shouts Sam, shocked at Robyn verbally assaulting Lizzy with such venomous rage.

Charity rushes to Robyn, trying desperately to calm her down, but she is inconsolable.

'How long have you known?' she yells, her body shaking violently, as Charity tries to sooth her, but she pushes her away, shouting hysterically, 'I trusted you, I trusted Lizzy, and it has all been a lie, a big dark lie.'

'No, it is not like that, we are all victims here, please try to understand and forgive,' says Charity, desperate to help her.

'It is all right for you, your father is from heaven, not from...' Robyn cannot finish the word, it is so abhorrent to her, as she turns on Lizzy, 'Your weakness caused this, if you had not succumbed, none of this would have happened, it is all your fault.'

'Succumbed to what? What is happening?' begs Sam now almost hysterical herself, as she sees her two dearest friends crumbling before her.

Lizzy pulls herself up from the floor, her body wretched with self-loathing at the torment she has caused her family the only thing that she lives for, and now she is hated.

'I did wrong, I wanted a child so much, but I have tried to do right by you, by my family. I love yah, my darling, please, please say you forgive me,' she begs clinging onto Robyn, as they watch, stupefied with disbelief at what is happening.

'My mother was violated and then condemned to rot in hell, and you ask for absolution. You ask for too much

cannot give it to you. I cannot look at you any more.
hate you. I hate what you have done. I hate what I am,'
he screams.

Charity and the others look on, desolate in their
mpotence to help, as Lizzy slumps to the floor, her heart
roken.

Robyn's words have destroyed her; she has ruined her
aughter's life and now Robyn's, there is nothing more
live for. She cannot come back from this. There is
owhere to go...

'I love yah, my darlings, remember that, I love yah...'

'Lizzy, oh my God, Lizzy, please do not go...' screams
harity

They rush to her, but it is too late.

Charity cradles her lifeless body in her arms, crying
ysterically, as Robyn stares, blankly into the air, while
e others stand, mummified with shock.

This cannot be. Their Lizzy is gone...

17

The Perfidious Spirit

They lay Lizzy's body on the grave of forgotten souls,
under the rainbow of ghost lights, which returns whenever
a wretched soul seeks peace. Each of them places their
own bulla upon her body, a secret prayer to guide her
on her journey to the heavens.

They form a circle around her, with lighted candles,
joining hands to enforce the RING'S golden light of love,
protecting her from the evil spirits that come in the night
to take her soul, as Charity stands in the centre with the
Book of Shadows. She opens it, as the rainbow of one
thousand ghost lights twinkle in the night skies and the
RING cry tears of sorrow for their beloved Lizzy, but
the one who cries the most is Robyn, whose damning
words crushed the life force from her.

Charity places a single tarot card in the centre of the
ring, the angel of forgiveness, as she casts the spell of
expulsion.

'I summon the magic of Grimoire
to arise from the pages of the gods.
I, she who is last,
release thy spirit.
♀
I release thee of guilt,

154

I release thee of pain,
I release thee of anguish.

♀

Let thy angel take thee to thy Lord.'

The book leaves her hand, floating above the card, as the spirits of the night whisper in the winds, while the earth beneath them rumbles with the sound of awakening souls. The card rises up from the ground, passing through the book, emerging on the other side as the Angel of Forgiveness.

She floats before them, with the golden ring of absolution around her head, majestic in golden robes of pure silk, as she spreads her magnificent gold and cream wings. She smiles, her soft voice floating in the night air, 'It is good to see you again, Charity, Charlotte is very proud of you.'

'Take care of my Lizzy, and tell her I will find Annie.'

'I will, Charity, be strong, be watchful, beware of false angels.'

The book returns to Charity, as the angel carries Lizzy into the night skies, to the rainbow of ghost lights, which lights the path to the heavens, as they watch her go to her Lord.

Kathy has laid the table with food, but inside her heart is sad, as Lizzy's sharp Irish brogue is nowhere to be heard. She did not care much for Lizzy, but in a strange way, she will miss her, this bossy, larger than life, tubby Irish woman, beloved by her family, who are now bereft with grief. As she serves the food, Jim prepares Fagan for Monty, who is so distraught that the only way he can release his pain is to ride through the night, until his body is spent.

He leaves them, unable to eat, looking coldly at Robyn, who stands alone in the corner of the drawing room, isolated and disconsolate, as everyone glares at her with silent rage.

Jack can take it no more, his body exploding with wrath, as he lashes out. 'You killed her, you bitch, our Lizzy. She loved you, cared for you, would give her life for you and you killed her...'

'I am sorry, I did not mean for her to die, I loved her, God help me, I loved her. Please, what am I to do? I cannot live with myself, help me, I do not know what to do.' She cries hysterically, while the others look on, coldly, unable to find it in their hearts to forgive her, everyone that is except Charity.

She feels Robyn's pain, understands her torment, and knows deep down in her soul, that it is not her fault, that something dark is controlling them, manipulating them like puppets.

'Stop it, stop it now. Lizzy killed Lizzy, not Robyn. She died through her own grief and guilt, which she carried with her for over forty years. Robyn is not responsible for that, anger did not kill Lizzy, the demon killed her, he is with us now, do not let him in, and do not let him destroy us. Fight him! We are a family, and we must remain strong and together if we are to win this battle.'

'But she said such terrible things to Lizzy, she broke her heart, we heard her, we saw it,' yells Sam, he eyes blood-red and puffy from crying.

'Yes, she was angry, yes, she said terrible things, but Lizzy told her terrible things. Any one of you would have reacted in the same way. We must learn to forgive each other, otherwise we are the beast that we are fighting, and that is what he wants. Do not let him into your souls; do not let darkness be your Lord. We are better than that. Lizzy was better than that, she would not want this...'

'I cannot bring her back, but I will try to understand why she lied and I will find my mother, for Lizzy,' cries Robyn, as Charity holds her in her arms, cradling her like a baby.

'We will go on for Lizzy's sake, but do not ask me to forgive you, because, right now I can just about tolerate being in the same room as you,' yells Jack, grabbing his coat and driving off into the night to drown his sorrows in the nearest pub.

Sam and Leo retire, leaving Robyn in the arms of Charity, who eventually persuades her to take a sleeping tablet, as she helps her to her room.

'You have the power to bring Lizzy to me, please Charity, let me see her, I need to see her, I need…'

'Shush, you must rest,' she says, helping her into bed. 'Lizzy knows that you love her, she is in a good place now, watching over us, but she needs time, time for herself. She needs to release her own demons, only then can she come to us. In time, my dear Robyn, you will see her again, but until then we must go on, we must find Annie and the third man…'

Robyn wipes her eyes, puffy red slits from constant crying, and her face pale and edged with deep sorrow lines, the face of a grief-stricken and wretched woman. It will be a long time before the sun enters her heart again, but Charity is right, she must go on, she must fulfil her promises to Lizzy, she must find her mother.

She falls asleep, as Charity makes her way to her room and an empty bed. Tonight she sleeps alone, as the grey spirits of Holmes House come out to taunt her, hissing, spitting and jeering, as they weave their way in and out of her body, whispering…

'He sees your ugliness, Charity, you cannot hide the beast, sleep the sleep of loneliness, for he leaves you soon.'

She is not in the mood for them tonight, 'Leave me be, or I will show you the terror of the beast,' she shouts, her body raging with anger, anger at the loss of her beloved Lizzy and anger at them, for deep inside she knows they are right.

But they do not care, as they continue to torment her, when, suddenly, she changes. Her rage has brought forth the beast, as Lilith flies at them, crushing them in her hands like spots of grey dust.

'Never taunt the beast, for it does not have a sense of humour,' she says, laughing, as the rest creep back into the walls, sheepishly.

She goes to the bathroom, checking her reflection in the mirror, as she sees Charity's face staring back at her, but with the body of a beast, a female beast, with wings and talons. She laughs, pruning herself, checking out her reflection, as Charity fights within to come back.

'Stop fighting me, Charity, are you not grateful that I dealt with those pitiful spirits? Let me help you, we are the power of two.'

'No we are not, I am Charity Holmes, not you, I control who I am, not you, I summon you, and you do not come without invitation,' she says, screaming at the mirror, as the two battle it out for control.

'I am Lilith, you do not summon me, I come when I choose. You have no choice, my soul is within you now, and we are as one.'

'But I cannot live like this; I will not let you take my life,' she rages.

'Your life was already mine the moment the Druid Vate summoned Hecate. Your blood is my blood, your body is my body, your spirit my spirit, and your soul, my soul. Accept what you are, Charity, do not fight me. I live through you and you through me; we are as one; neither controls the other, for neither can exist without the other.

158

'What do you mean?'

'If the body dies, the spirit dies, and if the spirit dies, the body dies. One cannot exist without the other, we are equal.'

She stands in front of the mirror, the beast and the woman staring back, both one and the same. Is this the way it is going to be? Charity's heart sinks, as the tears flow. The grey spirits of Holmes House were right; no man could desire such a creature...

Time floats by, as Charity glares at her reflection, praying that a miracle will happen, but the beast is still here, until, finally she accepts.

'I see the beast, but I feel the woman,' she says, as the beast slowly disappears and her body returns.

Now she understands. If she cannot control her rage, then she cannot control the beast. She must learn to use her rage and listen to the woman. Only then will the power of two truly be one...

Monty dismounts, exhausted, as he sits by the lake, while Fagan drinks the cool moon-kissed waters. All he can see is Lizzy's smiling face, laughing rapturously, as he hears her voice echoing in the cold night air. He cannot believe that she is gone, it is not fair, why her? She was an innocent no-nonsense Irish woman who lived for her family, washing, cooking and cleaning for them, tending to their every need, always there for them. She was the mother his mother could never be. He loved her and now she was gone. What kind of God would allow this to happen? She was His devoted disciple, and look how he repays her. He begins to wonder if this God of theirs is truly all-seeing, all-knowing and all-loving, or is he just another false angel? Who is this God that Charity and the RING have pledged their lives to in the quest for truth?

Their Lord would not have let his beloved Lizzy die...

Tomorrow he will wake up and all this will have been a dream, and Lizzy will be serving him breakfast, laughing and bossing him around...

He looks out onto the lake, its dark, cold waters luminescent with the moon's reflection, as the trees rustle in the wind and Fagan nudges him in the shoulder. How peaceful it is here, as time stands still, and the world outside this enchanting place seems far removed.

His eyes are drawn into the lake, as the moon undulates, forming a shape that slowly rises out from the darkness of the waters, a beautiful woman, naked, except for swan feathers covering her perfect breasts and hips. She floats towards him, her long white hair trailing down her back into the dark waters, a water wraith; a spirit who lives in the depths of the lake.

He cannot move, as she walks out of the water towards him, her smile bewitching. He feels the touch of her cold, soft body against his.

'Do not be sad, Monty, let me comfort you, let me soothe away your fears, let me fill you up with pleasure, let me inside you, let me love you like no other woman can,' she whispers, as he feels his body succumbing, luxuriating in the pleasure of her lovemaking, while Fagan neighs and tramples the ground, sensing that this beautiful water goddess is not what she seems.

The early morning sunrise shines down upon the lake as Monty feels Fagan's warm wet tongue on his face, and wakes to find himself half-naked, his clothes strewn across the wet morning grass. He feels terrible, he remembers the beautiful woman from the lake, but cannot bring himself to believe that he would betray Charity. It must have been a dream. He was distraught with the loss of Lizzy and his mind temporarily lost in the intoxicating mystical atmosphere of the lake, as the moon's reflection sent him into a deep hypnotic sleep.

160

He almost believes it, except that he cannot explain his half-naked body and the fact the dream felt real.

Kathy serves up breakfast, as everyone sits in stilted silence. They cannot eat, the food is good, but she is not Lizzy. Robyn can barely look up, for fear of seeing the sea of condemning eyes staring at her. Jack is so hung over that he can barely function, while Sam and Leo pick at their food like sparrows. Charity senses that something has happened to Monty, she sees the guilt in his eyes. The eyes do not lie. He looks away, he cannot speak to her; how he can tell her that he made love to a spirit?

Charity is the first to break the silence of melancholy. 'Lizzy is gone, but if we do not discharge our quest, her death will have been meaningless. We must go on and we must go on together, for Lizzy.'

'I agree, today is the beginning of new a chapter in the life of the RING. Lizzy will be its heart, the driving force that will lead us to the truth,' says Monty, trying hard to understand that Robyn must feel more wretched than they can ever imagine.

Jack pulls himself together, as he reaches out to Robyn, touching her hand with his. 'I did not mean those terrible things I said to you last night. Forgive me, I was upset, I know you loved Lizzy.'

Robyn breaks down; she could not bear it if her family rejected her, as Sam rushes to comfort her. 'It is OK, whatever happened between you and Lizzy, it is past, and she would want us to remain a family.'

They finish breakfast, quietly remembering her, but Charity can see the aura around them; it is a melting fusion of dark red, green, blue and black: Lucifer's colours. There is an evil presence amongst them, which is slowly eating away at them, destroying her family.

161

'It is time to journey to the edge of the antediluvian world, where I believe the prophecy, *Quatrain 77*, begins. However, before we set off on our final path, we must rid ourselves of Lucifer's perfidious spirit, which is hiding amongst us.'

'You are scaring me, what do you mean perfidious spirit?' asks Sam, clinging to Leo, who looks bewildered.

'We are getting close to the truth and to finding the third tentacle, Lucifer's dark angel, who came in the form of the beast, devouring the flesh of man, to become man. He has been amongst us for the past four hundred years ... since Dr Legan died. He was the first to be taken, the first of many perfidious spirits that walk this earth,' says Charity, her voice strangely distant.

Jack is lost. 'What is this third tentacle? I thought we were looking for the coming of the third Antichrist, not some mythical sea devil's tentacle?'

'And what is this perfidious spirit, Spud, which you say is hiding amongst us?' asks Monty, still unable to look her in the eye.

'I had a dream where our Lord came to me in the form of the peregrine falcon, who flew me through the chasm of time. He showed me the birth of Annie and Robyn, conceived through a dream by the demon incubus. I saw the burial of the one thousand forgotten souls and the birth of the withered child, taken by Dr Legan to Angel Hospital, which he built on the grave of one thousand souls.

'He was the Devil's soldier, collecting unwanted diseased bodies, one thousand men, women and children, born to die at the hands of the beast...'

She hesitates; the air is iniquitous, as she feels his presence. The dark one is amongst them, but he is not ready to show himself. He is waiting.

'Dr Legan gave himself to Satan in return for immortality,

162

collecting the vessels needed to give his master's third tentacle life, one thousand bodies for one thousand years of darkness...'

Robyn looks at her and sees; her gift has become stronger since the death of Lizzy.

'But why kill them if they were needed as vessels?' asks Sam, her face stone white.

'For a demon to become man he must eat the flesh of man, but one mortal is not enough to give life to this beast in the form of humankind. The more flesh of man he devours the greater his power and the longer his mortality on earth will be. One thousand souls beget one thousand years. Angel Hospital was Dr Legan's gift to his Lord. Where the third tentacle reached out from the underworld, in the form of the beast, to take the form of man through the flesh of man, so that the prophecy of one thousand years of darkness could begin...'

'So Dr Legan was not eaten by this beast like the other wretched souls, but possessed by him, becoming this perfidious spirit, who has wondered the earth ever since?'

'Partly, Sam, it is more complicated than that.'

'How do you mean, Spud?'

'The perfidious spirit is the spirit of the beast, who has become mortal through the flesh of man, but to remain on earth he must enter the body of a live and willing disciple. Dr Legan gave himself willingly, and so the Antichrist was born through him, the third tentacle, who became the third man, who is the third Antichrist.

'He became immortal through the reincarnation of the Antichrist in him; he never dies, he just shape-shifts into other bodies when his mortal host has served its purpose. Since his rebirth, four hundred years ago, the Antichrist has been spreading his seed of evil, colonizing the earth with perfidious spirits, smaller tentacles, forming spirits in his own likeness, willing soldiers who give themselves to him in return for the promise of being amongst the chosen ones when the one thousand years of darkness begins.

'Slowly, they have been permeating our world. They are cunning, treacherous and deceitful, insidious and invasive, corrupting humankind, gradually eating away at humanity, until, eventually, there will be nothing left except a rotten core. It is then that he will rise...'

The atmosphere is unnaturally calm, as Charity's words slowly enter their consciousness, where they once again come up against that disquieting feeling that there are no coincidences.

They have been pawns in a game where he always wins, controlling their every thought and action through his perfidious spirits, leading them along a path of his choosing. He has been moving amongst them for centuries, shape-shifting, and always one step ahead, manipulating them, leading them to exactly where he wants them to be.

They cannot stop him coming. He is already here...

18

The Sleeper

Charity looks at her family; one of them is false, a perfidious spirit, colonized by the third Antichrist. Her heart is breaking; one of the RING has given themselves over to the dark side.

She has the power to see into their souls, see their true selves, the power, which Lucifer fears, the one thing that can stop the rise of the third Antichrist and the beginning of the one thousand years of darkness.

'One of you has betrayed us, chosen the dark side in return for...'

Jack leaps off the chair, throwing it against the wall in a fit of rage. 'You are wrong, you have gone insane, these powers of yours have turned your mind,' he yells.

Everyone is anaesthetized, shocked to the core, as Jack paces up and down the kitchen, while Monty looks at Charity, who is rigid with wretchedness. He sees that what she says is true, that one of them is false, a disciple of the Antichrist, and that she must destroy them.

'You cannot believe what you are saying is true!' cries Sam. 'Lizzy's death has tipped you over the edge; you are not thinking clearly, you are seeing demons everywhere, even amongst your family.'

Charity holds back the tears, as she looks to Monty, who still carries the guilt of the water wraith in his eyes,

165

as she says, 'No, Sam, I am afraid it is true and I am sorry, but I must reveal this perfidious spirit and destroy it. I have no choice...'

Robyn says nothing, as she sits there quietly watching each of them.

Leo comforts Sam, as she continues to shout at Charity, who stands stilted and alone. Jack paces the kitchen floor, ranting to himself, while Monty sheepishly waits to see what Charity will do.

The RING, bound together through blood, friendship, love and trust, now broken by death and deceit. What is happening to them?

'All right then, reveal this perfidious spirit, because you are going to look pretty silly when it doesn't appear,' yells Sam.

Charity leads them into the hallway, where she draws a pentagram with white chalk, five points for five people, with her in the centre. Each stands at their point, looking at Charity, who already knows who is false, but she must draw them out, if she is to destroy it.

She holds the *Book of Shadows* in her hand, as she recites the spell of evacuation.

> *'I call thee out*
> *false spirit of the netherworld.*
> *Reveal thy self,*
> *thee cannot hide,*
> *thee cannot harm,*
> *thee cannot be bound by thy skin.*
> ♀
> *Let the bones of thy vessel awake.'*

The room is inaudibly still, as they wait. Sam smiles quietly to herself, as stillness turns to an eerie silence, the silence before the storm...

The pages of the book stir, turning over one by one, until eventually they stop, as Charity looks down to see a picture. It is a dagger, the dagger of requital, God's golden dagger, used by Charlotte to destroy Alex at the Final Reckoning. It rises out of the page, mesmerizing the RING, as it moves around the pentagram, stopping and pointing accusingly before each of them, as they gaze upon its ivory handle, carved in the shape of the sign of the cross, emblazoned with precious jewels.

Five times it circles the pentagram, each time passing by one of them, until there is only one left, the dagger suspended before them, pointing directly at their heart...

The RING are frozen in disbelief, as the dagger spins around, returning to the centre of the pentagram, suspended in front of Charity, its sharp blade pointing directly at, Leo...

Sam is desolate, as she looks to Charity and then Leo, who stands unmoved by the look of betrayal on her face.

'It is a mistake, tell them Leo, tell them that you are not this evil spirit, tell them Leo, please, tell them,' she begs, her body sick with consternation, as Robyn and Jack rush to her, grabbing her, as she crumbles to the ground.

'Why, Leo? Why?' she cries, looking up at him from the arms of Robyn, as he stares down at her, part of him destitute with grief at the pain he is causing her, but the other part, the spirit, cold and devoid of all emotion. The spirit and the man, but the man has long since been lost, sold to the devil for false promises. The others can barely comprehend that their friend was never really their friend at all, but a disciple of the Antichrist, who has spread his seed into the very heart of their world. How can they fight an enemy that they cannot see, whose camouflage lets him move so effortlessly from one mortal to another, becoming one of them with such terrifying ease?

'What turned you, Leo, what did the Antichrist offer you that was so alluring? I know you love Sam, I know you were a good man, I know you still feel remorse,' asks Charity, as the dagger slides into her right hand.

Robyn helps Sam up, as she looks into Leo's eyes, looking for the soul of the man she adores, the man she thought loved her with equal passion.

He turns away, unable to return her gaze, ashamed of what he has become; the man is still there, but only for a moment, as he says, 'The third millennium of darkness will soon be here, and then only those who have the protection of the Antichrist will survive, the rest will become his slaves. You cannot win, Charity, he knows and sees everything, he controls everything, and the world is already becoming his. Twenty-seven years will pass and then darkness will fall. He will rule over all for one thousand years, at the end of which the underworld will swallow it up, where the Lord of Darkness waits to receive it into his kingdom...'

'But you had Sam, you had us, you had power as a judge and the respect of your peers, you had the world at your feet. Why sacrifice all of that for a world of despair, where you are the slave and not your own master?'

'I was given those things,' he replies, turning back to look at Sam, who can no longer feel anything, her body numb with shock. 'I was going nowhere, my life was nothing, no future, no wife, no respect, just a boring nobody barrister, who no one noticed. Then he came. My saviour. He told me the truth, he showed me the real world and I saw the future, a world wreaked with havoc. There will be wars, many wars, all over the world, lasting twenty-seven years, leading to final annihilation ... and then the darkness will come.

'He gave me power and respect. I have a beautiful young wife, I move amongst the rich and powerful, I

168

influence people. I am one of the chosen ones. He is our saviour and you are the fools.'

Monty, Robyn and Jack cannot believe what they are hearing, this man cannot be the Leo they admired and respected. Sam looks at him. Where is the gentle, kind man who swept her off her feet, loved and protected her? No, this creature cannot be him, surely she would have seen through him?

'Was it all a lie, Leo, were you ever the man I fell in love with?' she asks, her voice weak and trembling.

He looks at her, and for a moment, the connection is there.

'You loved the man he made me, not the man I was before. He has the power to do that, to change people, make them what they want to be. I became all the things you wished for in a man, and so you believed in me. That is what he does. He is our saviour.'

'He is a false saviour, like the two before him, and he will be destroyed like they were,' says Charity, as she looks over at Sam, who knows what she must do. Sam nods back, their eyes acknowledging the pain of the other's torment.

Leo stands there, waiting, unafraid, knowing what his fate will be, for martyrdom, according to his master's decree, is the gateway to immortality in his kingdom. So he welcomes death, it holds no fear, as his rewards in his Lord's kingdom will be plentiful.

Charity releases her hand and the dagger flies towards him, striking him straight through the heart. His body disintegrates.

Sam walks away with the others, as the dagger returns to the book and Charity closes the page, which sealed the fate of Leo Francis.

'Did he have to die?' asks Jack, helping himself to a double Scotch, even though it is only ten o'clock in the morning.

169

'I had no choice, Jack, we could not trust him. He would have betrayed us when the time was due; he was a sleeper.'

'What do you mean a sleeper?' asks Sam, still numb, as Robyn comforts her, feeling her pain, two wretched souls together, their lives destroyed through deceit and lies by the two people they loved the most.

Charity's heart is heavy, as she looks at what is left of her family. Two people she loved are gone, one through guilt and the other through betrayal. She knows that this Antichrist is different, that he will not show himself like the others; he can wait, wait until man has destroyed man. He seeps into their thoughts; first there is the fear, fear of not being in control; then there is despair; then emptiness; and lastly, futility, the pointlessness of life – man destroying man.

Then he comes offering salvation...

She looks at Sam, her dearest friend, who has been her rock since childhood, and she had to destroy her husband. Leo was right, he is winning, he does control them, the balance has shifted, and she is not sure if it will ever be equal again.

'Charity, you did not answer my question,' says Sam, her voice cold and distant, their friendship now irrevocably damaged. In her soul, she knows that Leo had to go, but it still hurts that he had to die at the hands of her 'sister'. How can things ever be the same between them again?

'A sleeper,' she replies, pulling herself together. 'He is one of the many thousands of the Antichrist's disciples, the perfidious spirits, the seeds of the third tentacle, who live amongst us, who are us, but their thoughts are darker and more calculating, slowly affecting the equilibrium of our lives, our world. They are in positions of power: politicians, congressional representatives and judges like

170

Leo, all with the power to affect the balance of world policies. They are anarchists, terrorists and dictators or just simple people who fear the unstable world they live in, who are seeking refuge from their own fears.

'They are the weapons of the third Antichrist, feeding our fears and greed, only to lead us into damnation...'

'But if what you say is true, then we can never stop him, stop them; the beginning of the end has already begun,' says Robyn, her voice quiet and subdued, her spirit broken, her will destroyed. He is amongst them, eating away at their souls, the rot has begun.

'But Leo led us to the prophecy, *Quatrain 77*, the clue to the Antichrist, why lead us to him if he wanted to stop us?' asks Jack

'Do you not get it yet?' says Monty, as everything suddenly clicks.

'Get what?' he replies, agitated, as Charity explains.

'He wants us to find him, find the core of his world. He has been leading us to him all the time, controlling us, watching and waiting to see how powerful we really are. How powerful I am. He has been testing me, seeing whether I am equal to his dark powers, seeing whether the chosen one really is his nemesis.

The Spirit, his children, Alex and Lucy, the Patient, and Leo were all sent to test the chosen one, the one with the power of two,' she says, gripping Monty's hand tightly.

Sam sits up, her mind spinning, as she tries to understand what is happening to them. 'Are you saying that we have never been in control, that all this was meant to happen, that he knew his children would die, that we would save the Spirit and Patient, but lose Leo and Lizzy? That everything was just a game so that he could test you?'

Charity closes her eyes, trying to see her way through the maze that they are in, trying to let them see how it

171

is. 'That is what good and evil is about, Sam. The balance of power between the two is so fragile that it only takes the very slightest of movements to tip it over. There are two fundamental differences between good and evil, freedom and absolute rule. The good will always have a choice, the choice of free will, which our Lord bestowed upon man when He created him. We have the choice to choose who we are and what path we take. I have the choice to use my powers for good or evil, God will not choose it for me. He lets me go my own way, He guides, He watches, He protects and He loves, but He does not take away my freedom.

'However, evil has no choice, it hates to lose, it does not allow for failure, it will not allow free will for fear of failure. It manipulates and terrifies, destroying humankind's ability to think, the ability to choose. Lucifer sent his servants to test me, to see how far I would go to save their souls, but whether I win or lose, he wins. If I save them, he sees how powerful I am and so he is prepared. He knows who I am, my strengths and my weaknesses. He enjoys the game of power; he enjoys watching souls fight for their freedom; he enjoys watching me suffer as I lose myself along the way, torture myself with doubts and fears, see my family torn apart, through lies and betrayal. He enjoys watching the destruction of all that is good in the fight against evil. He exists to destroy.

'Evil has no limits, the Lord of Darkness has no limits, and he is remorseless in his pursuit of absolute power. The prophecy, *Quatrain 77*, is almost upon us, and so he needs to finish it; the game must end, but in a place of his resurrection...'

19

The Edge of the Antediluvian World

'Where is this place?' asks Monty, knowing that when they get there, win or lose, they have already lost.

Charity looks at him and sees that Lucifer will use him to stop her, that he will be her nemesis. 'The edge of the antediluvian world... where two worlds, the underworld and ours, will collide into one, where the definitive battle between good and evil shall be our final denouement...'

'But what about Annie, we must find her, or is that another trap?' asks Robyn.

'Everything we do is watched from the two opposing worlds of spirit – the dark and light – looking to see who will win the battle of good versus evil; angels and demons, spirits and mortals, crossing over into each other's spheres, battling it out for control, seeking power over their own destinies.

'Lucifer holds Annie to him, knowing that we will come, but that does not mean that she is false; her fate is real. God let her go so that she would lead us to him, and Lucifer, knowing this, sent the beast to take her; the balance of the game of good against evil is unending.'

'How will we find Annie and this place where the end of the world begins?' asks Robyn.

'It is time to call upon the power of two, to use my gift through the *Book of Shadows*, to call upon my ancestors, who wait for my command. It is time to know who I really am...'

'What do you need from us?' says Sam, trying to be strong, looking beyond her own pain, into the abyss of the underworld, Leo's world, which, if they lose, becomes their world...

'I need you to believe in me, in our quest and in our Lord. I need you to know that we are still the RING, and always will be, no matter what the end may bring. I need your strength and love; if I have that, then I am ready...'

One by one, they look at each other, that silent, unwavering look of amity between friends that says everything.

The time has come when destiny calls...

'Before we journey to the edge of the antediluvian world I need to ask a question that only the angels can answer, and I need to ask it alone.'

Monty does not ask why, he just looks at her tenderly, as she leaves them to prepare for their final journey. She walks, alone, along the path at the back of Holmes House, which leads to the woods of whispering trees, where folklore tells that if you make a wish when the silence comes, the woods will grant it.

The trees whisper, as the winds rustle lightly through the branches, while the birds' mystical harmony resounds through the dense woodland, defining in their calls to each other. Charity finds herself standing in a glade of thick green grass, surrounded by trees, a circle of tall, dark trees, which form a wall around the glade, protecting it from outsiders.

She stands in the middle of the glade, waiting, until she hears it... silence, the soundlessness of tranquillity, as she closes her eyes and wishes. She can feel the sunlight on her face, and the warmth of the heavens, as she opens her eyes. Finally they have come, Ma and Pa. She sees them floating towards her, her guardians; Ma, a vision of pure white translucent light, and Pa with his magnificent pale-blue wings and blond hair. Her heart lifts. Oh how she has missed them, as they wrap their wings around her, cocooning her in their protective embrace.

'Our precious daughter, so brave and yet so alone. We heard your prayers, daughter, but we could not answer,' says Ma, caressing her face with her soft luminous hand.

'Why, Ma, why can you not help me when I need you the most? Why forsake me when I call to you during the nightmare of my dreams? How cruel is our Lord to keep you from me, when He sends me into battle with the darkest of enemies,' she cries, as her father is silent.

'We cannot impede, my darling; you must make this final journey on your own,' she replies, while Charity looks to her father, as he circles the glade, avoiding her gaze.

'But you are my guardians; you have always protected me, what is different now? I need to know the truth, tell me the truth or I cannot go on,' she yells, her voice trembling.

'It is time to tell her, Metatron,' says Ma, looking at her father, who is floating in the middle of the glade, his handsome face glowing.

'Metatron, I know that name from somewhere,' says Charity.

'Have you ever wondered why I had no name, Charity, why your mother had a past, but I did not. I just existed, your father, whose name was never spoken, except as Pa. Did you ever wonder, my daughter, why this was?' he says, his voice soft and loving, the voice of a father with a secret, but with a love for his daughter that surpasses all other loves.

She looks at him and sees that he is different; he is

175

changing, his face dividing into four and his wings into six, with a halo of four rings radiating from him. Four golden lights of blinding colour; blue, red, green and yellow, the colours of the gods: Eurius, air; Notus, fire; Zephyrus; water and Boreas, earth – lords of the four elements.

His robes are sumptuous in matching colours, and his wings, the colour of the heavens, white and gold, the wings of a supreme and infinite personal being, a seraphim. One of God's four holy beasts, as listed in the Book of Revelation, who give off a light so intense that not even other divine beings may look upon it without being blinded by its purity.

His faces, depict the four gods of time: the handsome youth Eurius; the young warrior Notus; the middle-aged man Zephyrus; and the wise old man Boreas. But for a moment he becomes Pa again.

'Do not look upon my light, Charity, but above my being to the heavens, for if you gaze into the light of a seraphim, the eclipse of darkness will be your fate,' he says, as she covers her eyes with her arm, while Ma glides towards her, shielding her from the blinding light with her wings.

'Do not cry, my daughter,' he says, as she wipes away the tears.

'I see who you are. I know the legend of the seraphim – four angelic beings, created by God to watch over mankind, one of whom was called Metatron, chief of the ministering angels, highest of his celestial hierarchy, and patriarch of the antediluvian world,' she says.

Her thoughts go back in time, as she remembers wondering why her father had no name, how, even at the Final Reckoning, when his soul was exalted into the heavens, as an angel, she never knew his name. It was always there, a niggling doubt that whenever they spoke,

176

his name was never mentioned, that he was always just Pa.

'I see your thoughts, my daughter, and now you shall know why,' he says, raising his arms up to the heavens, bringing forth the vision of his past...

A handsome mortal, who once wandered the earth in ancient times, ending his journey at the edge of the antediluvian world; a dark, cold place, where darkness eclipsed daylight. There he became the paterfamilias of his people, a seer who worshipped the Druid ways, but whose goodness was so legendary that when he died and entered the heavens God honoured him with the role of seraphim.

He named him Metatron, the angel of fire, whose light can eclipse all darkness, the watchtower of earth and the keeper of the souls who wander among the antediluvian world.

The vision disappears, and Charity, at last, understands.

'Long before Nostradamus saw the coming of the third Antichrist I, the patriarch of the Druid seers, saw the darkness, which would come to a world and place where my journey of time was destined to end – the antediluvian world.

'I saw the birth of a child, my child, which would be the salvation of the world, but in that vision, I also saw the coming of the third Antichrist, Lucifer's dark angel, who would come in the guise of a false saviour. He would be the most evil and cunning of beasts, wandering the earth, corrupting all that he touched, until he, like I, would end his journey at the edge of the antediluvian world.

'When I entered the heavens, God gave me the gift of fatherhood. I returned to earth and took the form of man to give life to you, my beloved daughter. You are the child of Metatron, the last great Druid seer and God's

177

supreme angel, born with the gift of sight, the power of the angels and the Druids' ancient shamanic powers of the shape-shifter.'

'Why not tell me the lineage of my birth, why the secrecy and why did you die at the hands of Lucifer's assassin when you had the power to destroy him? Why enter the fires of hell when you could have returned to your rightful place in the heavens?'

'To fight the beast we must sometimes enter its jaws, become it in order to overcome it. Lucifer's weakness is that he believes all beings, mortal and spirits, are corruptible, as he was, therefore he could not see a false angel within his own kingdom. Evil cannot see beyond its own darkness, its own arrogance; it always thinks it is smarter than good, because good does not destroy to win.

'God knew that he would seek you out, try to destroy you before the coming of his evil servant, the beast who is in his own likeness. My death was his weapon. From within Lucifer's kingdom I saw into the soul of the beast, understood his mind and so became like him, protecting you, until you saved me, when he sent the Spirit to trap you.

'You have proved to be a mighty adversary, as his time runs out, and your powers grow stronger.'

'But I still do not understand why you and Ma abandoned me, let me fight this war on my own, and let Lizzy die, and Annie's soul be taken, when you could have saved them?'

'The world of darkness plays by no rules, but you have the power of two within you, the angel and the beast. But only one can enter the heavens. Should we help you before you reach your journey's end, then the beast has right of passage to our Lord's kingdom, which cannot be.'

178

'But you gave me the power of the beast, I did not choose to be born like this, so why punish me for your creation? I am in your likeness, father,' she says, angrily.

'Every child is born bearing the seeds of its parents; choice only begins when first breath is taken. You can choose to go on or turn away, and our Lord will understand, but you are the daughter of Metatron, God's supreme seraphim and the elder of the Druids. Your blood is that of Hecate, the triple goddess of the underworld, and your earth mother Mary. You possess the soul of Lilith, the beast with the power of the witch's dark magic.

'You are the first supreme supernatural being, born of mortal flesh, with the power of light and dark, whose soul is that of the beast, but whose essence is of the angels. You are Lucifer's nemesis...'

Charity is in turmoil, her body racing with rage at being born with such powers, which have brought more pain than joy, yet she is her father's daughter, whose whole being is pureness. She cannot turn away.

'I will go on, Pa. You say I have a choice, but inside I feel I do not. I must do what destiny dictates.'

'You did choose, my daughter, for the beast in you filled you with rage, trying to turn you away, but goodness won through. You chose the side of light.'

'What about Annie?'

'She waits for you and you shall see her again,' he says, as Ma returns to his side and they ascend to the heavens.

Charity watches them go, as she cries out, 'Will I see you again?' feeling that this will be the last time that they will all be together. They are gone, but she hears their voices whispering in the trees:

'Look for us in your third-eye, Charity; we will always be there...'

179

'Did you get the answer you wanted?' asks Monty, as she walks into the bedroom to find him sitting on the edge of the bed, in solemn thought, his hands covering his face.

'I keep thinking of the words of the Emulating Soul, "You cannot go back, when the three become one; you cannot go back,"' she replies, looking at him, as the two of them feel the touch of perdition.

'I am guilty of betrayal, my love,' he says, reaching up and touching her hand, as she looks into his eyes, the eyes of a wretched man. 'When I rode out into the night after Lizzy's funeral, I was bewitched by a water wraith, who seduced me and we made love. I betrayed our love, I...'

'Shush, honey,' she whispers, pulling him to her, feeling his pain. 'The devil sends his demons when your heart, soul and body are broken, when you are destroyed. He uses your grief to take your goodness. Evil plays upon fear and despondency, sucking you into its darkness under the illusion of blissfulness and the offer of salvation from your despair. We must not let him destroy our love through your guilt and my anger, which is what he wants, to weaken our biggest weapon against him, our belief in each other.'

They lose themselves in each other's bodies, loving each other with such passion, that they melt into one being. Whatever world awaits them out there, they will always have this moment, captured, and forever theirs...

Kathy serves dinner before leaving for a night out with Jim, the house empty except for the RING. Even the spirits remain hidden, as they eat their food in quietude, silently reflecting. Robyn thinking about Annie and Lizzy, and her 'father', and what manner of beast is silently

180

lurking within her. Jack, who never speaks of his family, or any past loves, a solitary man, with secrets of his own, which even now he closes his mind to, choosing only to think of the moment. Sam, who always loses the ones she loves – her father, mother and two husbands. Everyone dies on her; will today be the same? Monty, the cool aristocrat with a dark family past, who never really knew about affection or real love until Charity, and now he may never know it again after today. And then Charity, the Inceptor, the chosen one, whose whole life has been one long journey of dark secrets, lies, betrayal and love. Would she live this life again, the pain, the loss, the tears, the joy, the laughter, the excitement, the challenges and the passion?

To feel everything is better than to feel nothing. Each day has been an adventure, each quest a revelation and each battle intoxicatingly exhilarating. Yes, she would do it all again...

The clock strikes midnight and the house feels unnaturally quiet, as they look at each other, waiting, no one prepared to say the words, which will send them into the abyss of darkness...

'It is time,' says Charity, finally forcing herself to speak.

'We are ready if you are, Spud,' says Monty, as they follow her out into the walled garden, a beautiful restored garden, protected by a high wall. In the centre is a circle of flowers, that, under the light of a full moon, forms the outer circle of a pentagram. As they look into it, they see the five points.

'I have lived here all my life, yet I never noticed this before,' says Monty, transfixed by the pentagram.

'Your ancestors used this when practising their Satanic rituals. It is only visible at midnight, and to the one who possesses the witch's magic,' says Charity, placing the *Book of Shadows* in the centre, the sacred space, while

181

signalling to each of them to seal the cardinal points, protecting the inner circle.

The air is still as she calls upon the magic of the book, casting the spell of invocation, calling the spirit Lilith into her.

> *'I call upon the spirit of the beast*
> *to rise up from the darkness,*
> *to enter thy soul.*
> ♀
> *To become one*
> *in the power of two.'*

The moon shines down upon the book, which opens, as the pages turn, flicking through the magic of the gods, until the beast Lilith is laid bare, as she breathes the air of life, ascending from the book, suspended in all her ugliness before them. Her wings cast high behind her, as she flexes her talons and looks to Charity, who repeats the spell of invocation, drawing the beast into her, as it flies towards her, merging into her body, until they are one.

The power of the beast is awoken. Monty and the RING gaze in horrified wonderment at Charity, who stands before them, part woman, part creature, the face of an angel and the body of a beast.

The beast flaps her wings, as she turns to look at Monty, who does not recoil like last time in the crypt, but smiles back, as Charity acknowledges his love, while the pages of the book keep turning until it closes.

'Do not be afraid at what you see, but trust in the power of the beast's magic, which will guide us to the edge of the antediluvian world, and the definitive battle,' she says, casting the final spell, which will send them into the world of darkness...

> *'I, she who is last,*
> *command the power of Grimoire*
> *to open the gateway of universal space.*
> ♀
> *Let the magic of Grimoire*
> *protect thee and thy servants*
> *and show thee the way.'*

The earth shakes beneath them, as the moon eclipses into the colour of blood and the night sky explodes into an electrifying thunderstorm, which charges through their bodies, lighting up the circle. Red bolts of light fly out from the centre of the moon, striking through the heart of the book, which combusts into flames, causing the earth beneath to erupt, opening up into a volcanic mass of red-hot lava, expelling vile smelling gases, as the book disappears into the burning void of smelting earth.

The ground opens up into a flaming pit of fire, which swallows the RING into it, their bodies becoming human rods of light, sinking further and further into the pit of volcanic flames. They feel nothing, no fear, no pain, as they descend into the earth, submerged into the fires of hell, disappearing into the underworld, which becomes darker and colder the deeper they go, as the fires turn to black earth and their bodies return to mortal flesh.

They are in a tunnel of darkness, their bodies spinning in a black hole that seems bottomless, as they tumble down into the ends of the earth. Suddenly they see a light hurtling towards them from out of the blackness, careering into them, lifting them up out of the grip of the underworld into the antediluvian world.

It is freezing cold and pitch black, as they pull themselves together, their bodies shivering from the icy air, which freezes their breath, as they rub their hands together, desperately trying to keep warm, while stomping their feet, which feel like frozen lumps of ice.

'Where are we? It cannot be hell, it is too bloody cold?' says Jack, blowing his fingertips in a vain attempt to put life back into them, as they turn purple.

'Look, look at the sky, it's changing colour,' shouts Sam, as they look up into the blackness to see shimmering curtains and bands of light, flipping and waving through the sky, a melting pot of greens, purple and red.

'Aurora borealis,' says Charity, flexing her wings, the beast impervious to the cold, as they look up in wonderment at the brilliant, almost super-terrestrial lights, which cover the entire sky, lifting the world of darkness into the heavens.

'We are in northern Alaska,' shouts Monty.

'The northern lights, aurora borealis,' says Charity, repeating the words again, as they are all hypnotized by the mystical display of glimmering lights.

'But what has Alaska to do with the third Antichrist? I mean he comes from the fires of hell, so what has the coldest country on earth got to do with the coming of the King of Terror?' asks Robyn, who cannot fathom it out, yet knows that this is where it all begins.

Charity finally understands Nostradamus's prophecy, *Quatrain 77*, it all makes sense now, now that she is here, at the edge of the antediluvian world. 'I see it all,' she says.

'See what, Spud?' asks Monty, feeling strange talking to this grotesque beast standing beside him, as the night sky covers them in light.

'*Quatrain 77*, I understand it now,' she replies, quoting it again:

> '*The Antichrist very soon annihilates the three;*
> *Seven and twenty years his war will endure,*

184

The heretics are dead, imprisoned, exiled,
Red hail, water, blood and corpses cover the earth.'

They all look at her, as she laughs, the beast flapping its huge grey wings and flying up into the sky, its shadow reflecting against the brilliant aurora's lights, while it flips and turns in the sky, its ugly body strangely beautiful against the heavenly lights of aurora borealis.

Finally, she swoops down, standing proudly in front of them, as she reveals the coming of the third Antichrist.

'The world will be in turmoil, the Antichrist's sleepers, the perfidious spirits, worming their way through humankind, affecting everything, the balance of nature, our thoughts, our fears, our greed, turning man against man, leading them into the paths of spiritual destruction and ultimately damnation.

'It has already begun, each tentacle spreading out, forming the 'seven signs', as written in the Old Testament: religious wars; internal revolutions; worldwide war; famine; the poisoning of the earth; earthquakes; plagues and disease.

'These will last twenty-seven years, starting from the Middle East, invading through Europe, culminating in the third world war, leading to the annihilation of humankind. The twin towers, America, East Africa, England, every country affected, the world affected, through terrorism and internal destruction, the perfidious spirits, the tentacles, spreading the Antichrist's poison, eating away at the very nucleus of world policies.

'Finally, at the end of twenty-seven years of world disasters and wars, darkness will descend, when the Antichrist, Lucifer's third tentacle, will come. He will rule for one thousand years, the earth in total darkness, humankind his servants, the heretics dead, imprisoned or exiled and the earth covered in blood and corpses.'

They watch, mouths opened in stunned stupor, as Charity and beast show them the future, a dark, empty and soulless world, where the demons rule over man, where Lucifer and his court of dark angels spread their evil like a black curtain, which eclipses all light, extinguishing the very essence of humankind – hope...

'But I still do not understand where Alaska enters this dark world, why it all begins from here?' asks Robyn, her voice trembling with fear.

The beast bends down, stroking Robyn's face with her sharp talons, as Charity smiles, saying, 'The balance of nature: we are at the extreme point of northern Alaska, where the sun sets at noon on 18th November every year and does not show again until midday on 24th January, the winter solstice, where the sun does not rise for sixty-seven consecutive days, where there is nil hours of sunlight. It is during this time that the skies are sometimes lit up with a celestial phenomenon, bands and curtains of coloured lights, spellbinding lights known as aurora borealis, the northern lights of Alaska.

'The sun gives off high-energy charged particles known as ions, which travel out into space at speeds of three hundred to twelve thousand kilometres per second, forming a cloud known as plasma. This plasma travels like a stream from the sun (the solar wind), which interacts with the edge of the earth's magnetic field (the edge of the ante-diluvian world), trapping it, forcing it down into the ionosphere, earth's atmosphere. The particles collide with gases from the ionosphere, causing them to glow, producing the celestial lights, aurora borealis.

'The lights are constantly in motion, due to the changing interaction between the solar wind and the earth's magnetic field, generating up to one million megawatts of electricity, which interferes with power lines, radio and satellite communications.'

She stops, looking up at the lights, then out into the darkness, before turning to the RING...

'What if this delicate phenomenon of nature were altered, its balance tipped over the edge, changing the earth's atmosphere, causing darkness to creep into the world like a veil, slowly covering the earth, obliterating light forever?'

They listen, frozen to the core, not from the cold, but at her last words, 'obliterating light forever', as Monty asks the question that everyone fears.

'How?'

The beast swings round; they are standing at the top of a black mountain, looking out into the abyss of darkness, the edge of the antediluvian world, with only the aurora borealis lighting the way. She tells them how the Lord of Darkness will turn our world into his, twin earth's atmosphere with the underworld, drawing two worlds into one. 'It will begin slowly, the world in turmoil, man fighting man, unable to see the balance shifting, tipping over into the side of darkness.

'Imagine a world where there's three hundred and sixty-five days of sunlight, where, in that time, at the edge of the antediluvian world, sixty-seven days are in darkness, leaving two hundred and ninety-eight days of sunlight.

'Each year, for the next twenty-seven years, the balance slowly shifts. Every year in northern Alaska there will be an extra eleven days of darkness at the winter solstice, five before 18th November and six after 24th January, until the twenty-seventh year, when the antediluvian world – Alaska – has three hundred and sixty-five days of darkness, and no sunlight...

'Then, he will come... The third Antichrist. The curtain of darkness will spread out from the edge, covering the world, until, sunlight is obliterated, and the one thousand years of darkness begins...'

187

The icy air fills with their breath, heavy puffs of panic, as their hearts beat faster and the adrenalin races through their blood.

No, this is not possible. The world would notice these dramatic changes. Alaska would do something about it. They would come up with a solution.

They would stop it...

20

The Cephalopod

The ground oscillates beneath them, trembling, causing the mountain to erupt into a black volcanic mass, an earthquake, as it opens up, and sucks them into it. They desperately cling onto the top, but the earth crumbles in their hands, as they slowly slide further and further down into the bottomless pit of darkness.

Charity flies up, the beast flapping its mighty wings, suspended, picking them up one by one with her powerful talons, carrying them to safety, away from the black mountain, to the other side of the lake, as they watch it spit out its poisonous, foul-smelling black gases and red flames. The aurora borealis is blackened by the fumes of the boiling lava, which pours out of the mountain and down into the icy lake, turning it into a black sludge of hot, spitting volcanic mud.

It appears...

Long, black, rubbery tentacles slide over the top of the void, gripping the sides of the mountain, 30 feet of soft slippery flesh with huge suckers at the end, pulling their host out of its lair, lifting its slimy body to reveal ... the Cephalopod, the devil-octopus, half beast, half octopus, dark creature of the underworld; Lucifer in his truest form, the evil organism, the host octopus whose tentacles reach out and destroy everything they touch.

189

He is the ugliest of creatures, with a huge black horned head, red Satanic eyes, vampire teeth, pointed ears and large proboscis; his body is muscular and powerful like the beast, but slimy and flexible as an octopus, with the Devil's wings folded behind him.

The Cephalopod: the most highly developed of all marine molluscs, the squid, whose brain is fully functional at birth and whose eyesight can see into the dark. Their bodies can change colour and shape, and can even squeeze through a hole the size of a dime. They move by squirting liquid from their body, jet-propelling from one place to the next and destroying predators with toxic black ink. They can pick an enemy up with their suckers and crush them with their tentacles, which can slide and crawl into any crevice.

Lucifer, the devil-octopus, evil personified, the creature of the underworld who cannot die, whose eight tentacles reproduce every time they are destroyed.

He sits on top of the volcano, his tentacles spread out slithering down the mountain, seven 30-foot lethal weapons protecting their host, Lucifer, whose grotesque black body looks down upon them.

'So you finally made it to my lair, Charity. Welcome, I have been waiting for this time, beast against beast, the definitive battle,' he says, his dark voice echoing through the black Alaskan skies.

'Do not move,' she says to the RING, 'this battle must be fought between us, and the winner takes all.'

'But we are in this together, we fight him together,' shouts Monty, angry and afraid, his body trembling uncontrollably from fear and cold, as the others cannot move, their whole being trapped inside their own fear.

The beast bends down to caress her lover, as he feels the touch of her talons running over his body and her wings wrapping themselves around him. Charity whispers,

190

'You cannot win this one, honey, only I can, it is destined, it is my fate. It is the future...'

She flaps her wings, flying up into the air, turning round and looking down upon her family, as their eyes lock, Monty, Robyn, Sam and Jack, who see that this is the time, the definitive battle. Everything has been leading to this place, his lair: the edge of the antediluvian world.

There are no coincidences, only destinies...

She spreads her magnificent wings, flexing her talons, preparing for battle.

'There can be only one supreme ruler, and he is not you,' she shouts, as his evil laugh deafens them, while he calls his tentacles to him, seven mighty killing machines slithering and sliding in the air, their suckers ready to strike.

Charity flies towards him, her talons and teeth bared, as he waits, calmly, smiling, until she is almost there, when it appears, the eighth tentacle...

She stops in mid flight, horrified; it is a woman, captured in its deadly grip, as it rises out of the volcano into the air, dangling its prey before her: Annie...

'See what gifts I bring you, Charity, see how generous I am, how I wish to unite you with your loving sister,' he says, as she feels his slimy voice crawling all over her, her body transfixed with the sight of Annie swinging in the cold, black air, her reflection magnified against the aurora skies, his tentacle one inch away from crushing the life force from her.

'You cannot win, Charity, the twenty-seven years has already begun; my servant, the third Antichrist is already here. You will never find him, he is everyone and no one, shape-shifting through your world, preparing the way for my coming. His disciples multiply as I speak and the world is already in chaos, my tentacles are everywhere, invading every particle of your world, humankind and

191

nature, implementing the seven signs leading to the one thousand years of darkness.'

He swings his eighth tentacle around, laughing, as Annie cries out in despair.

'You cannot win, Charity, humankind will destroy itself, darkness is stronger than light. Your God cannot protect you from yourself; man will destroy man.'

'The balance will be kept and you will crawl back into your pit, your hovel of slime where you belong,' she replies, flying towards Annie, as their eyes lock into each other's souls, and they see each other's pain.

'Go back, Charity, go back, I am already lost,' she cries, as Charity rips into his tentacle, her teeth tearing at its rubbery flesh, drawing black poisonous blood, which trickles down into the burning black sludge of spitting mud.

He swings his tentacle around, commanding the others to join ranks, as they swiftly move in towards Charity. Lilith, the beast, swings through the air, her wings keeping her afloat, as she tries to release Annie by tearing his tentacle apart, while Robyn looks on, praying for her mother and mentor.

His seven tentacles grip Charity in their slimy embrace, as Annie is released, falling, screaming, towards the lake of volcanic mud, when Charity uses her shamanic powers, shape-shifting into an eagle, who slips through the tentacles, picking up Annie and flying her to Robyn. His eight tentacles follow them through the black air, past the eagle towards Monty...

His huge suckers pick him up, while the others turn to the eagle and Annie, coiling their tentacles around them, crushing them, as the eagle loses strength, its body tumbling to the ground, leaving Annie behind.

Now he has two, Annie and Monty...

Charity is beaten, as the eagle returns to the beast, it

wings broken, its talons bleeding and its teeth knocked out by Lucifer's powerful suckers. She looks up into the aurora's lights to see Annie and Monty gripped in the dark embrace of Lucifer's tentacles, which slither and slide in the skies, as he laughs, his body pulsating with arrogance and power.

'You cannot win, Charity, whatever shape you take. I am the ultimate beast, indestructible. Concede now and I will save your pitiful family; let them live for a little while longer, until my coming.'

'Do not listen to him, Charity, fight him, he cannot win,' shouts Monty, his bones cracking with the deadly embrace, as Annie cries out:

'Use the power of the three.'

Charity calls to the gods, raising the pellar's black athame to the skies, its magic sending bolts of lightning to the heavens, as she casts the spell of invocation, summoning the triple goddess into her.

'I summon thy mother,
dark goddess of the underworld
to come into thee
to give thee the power of three.'

The Aurora lights change colours, to black, green and red, while thunderclaps of lightning burst out from the sky, striking into Lucifer's tentacles, as they recoil in pain, slithering back into their lair, taking Annie and Monty with them.

Lucifer attacks, his eyes ejecting flames of fire, as the two forces collide, the skies aflame with the fires of demonic light, while Charity's body metamorphoses into Hecate, the triple goddess of the underworld.

She rises up from the ashes of black earth, the three-headed queen of black magic: Hecate, Queen of the

Underworld; Selene, moon goddess; and Artemis, goddess of the earth...

She is magnificent, her three heads twisting and turning in the skies: the owl, whose large eyes can see into the dark; the skeleton, whose kiss can turn its prey into bones; and the bat, whose bite can suck the life force from you. Her wings span the entire mountain, black bat wings, webbed together with the fingers of fallen angels. Her body, beautiful, with bare, soft, round breasts and long legs that end in sharp claws. Her six arms float in the air, her fingers serpent's fangs, with each bite more deadly than the other, as their venom paralyses, then kills.

The RING look like matchstick people, as she towers above them, her powerful heads swinging down and moving amongst them.

'Now we shall see whose magic is the greater,' she says, lifting herself up into the skies, flexing her wings, as she and Lucifer lock horns...

Lucifer sends out six tentacles, keeping Annie and Monty locked in the embrace of the other two, imprisoned in his lair, choking on the smelting earth and fires.

Annie's spirit is a frail, translucent light, her face old and wretched, bearing the tortures of twelve years imprisoned in the dark life, at the mercy of Lucifer. Her long hair is grey and thin, and her body wizened without her soul, which Lucifer holds to him, slowly destroying the essence of her goodness, torturing her with false hopes of freedom.

Monty looks at this tragic spirit, thinking that this cannot be Charity's sister, who died so young and looks so old. Is this to be his fate? He feels Lucifer's tentacle crushing the life force from him, as Annie looks over her weak, grey spirit almost disappearing into the darkness too frail to speak, yet her dark, soulless eyes say it all..

These two souls are locked together in the devil-octopus'

deadly embrace, awaiting their fate, as the beasts above battle it out to the death...

'Your soul belongs to the beast now, Charity, and there is no going back...' Lucifer commands, his eyes burning into her flesh, the flames of hell branding her, as the triple goddess looks down to see his mark, † engraved across her chest.

The pain is indescribable, as the three cry out in agony, screeching their howls of rage. He lifts his black, repulsive, octopus body out of his lair, spurting foul black liquid, as he spreads his wings and jet-propels his way towards her, his tentacles flying in the air, searching for its prey.

She spreads her wings, obliterating the aurora lights, as the owl sees through the darkness, leading the other two heads towards him. The two beasts clash in the skies, the devil-octopus and the triple goddess, tearing at each other, as their mighty bat wings flap in the air, causing currents of wind, blowing frozen water down onto the RING, who watch, helpless, their bodies fighting to stay on the ground, as the icy winds cut through them like a sword.

Lucifer curls his tentacles around the goddess, crushing the three heads into one fleshy mess, as the bat and the skeleton tear at his flesh, while her serpent's fingers bite into the tentacles, drawing black blood, paralysing them with their venom. His blood, more deadly than theirs, the serpents wither instantly, while the bat and the skeleton slowly die. His demonic blood races through them, sending them into madness with its poison, while their flesh disintegrates under the pressure of his tentacles.

'She is losing, they are lost, all of them, Charity, Monty Annie; he has them all and soon he will come for us,' screams Sam, as Jack and Robyn pray for a miracle.

His tentacles crush the goddess, as he laughs aloud,

while bringing up Annie and Monty from his lair, floating them in front of her, as they watch him slowly extinguish her...

Her body almost gone, the beast leaves, as Charity returns, shape-shifting back to the Inceptor, gripped in the octopus's tentacles. She looks at Monty and Annie, their eyes desperate, their fate almost upon them...

'You are mine now, Charity, I have you all, the prophecy will be fulfilled and your world will be mine,' he commands, as he slithers back to his lair, taking his prey with him, his tentacles swinging them back and forth, like rag dolls.

Annie, Monty, Charity, lost to the devil-octopus...

They look down into the black sludge of volcanic mud, which seems infinitely preferable to the fate that awaits them in Lucifer's underworld.

Charity knows she has lost, her soul is his, the penitent gate in her vision awaits her, she knew it was coming. She looks to Robyn, a distant ant-like figure, as she throws her the athame, and Lucifer returns into his lair, crawling back into the darkness, leaving the others behind, savouring their deaths for another day.

The earth begins to close in on them, as Lucifer drags them down into the pit of despair, the dark life, while Charity clings onto her necklace, her last hope. Too weak to speak, she casts the spell of Invocation in her mind's-eye, calling the rope of human spirits to life, one last time...

'I, she who is last, command thy spirits
to rise up from the ashes of blackness
and take thy servants to freedom.
♀
I release thee from thy charge
and offer mine self as sacrifice.'

196

She throws the necklace into the pit, as the spirits come to life, hundreds of tiny luminescent bats, who eat away at the tentacles holding Annie and Monty. Lucifer's black poisonous blood is useless against them.

They eat at the flesh until it's bone, freeing Annie and then Monty, flying them up, past Charity, who looks at them, as Monty cries out, 'Please do not leave me, Spud, I need you, I love you.'

The tears flow like a flood, his voice weak and desperate, as he watches her go, sinking down into the underworld, while the bats carry Annie and him out of the pit, and into the arms of their friends.

'Where is Charity, why is she not with you?' screams Robyn, as Monty collapses, a broken man, lost without his love. Annie takes hold of Robyn, her spirit released, her soul free, as she whispers:

'You will see her again, my beloved daughter. The beast will never hold her to him forever. She is her father's daughter...'

'But she is the Inceptor, the chosen one, she was born to stop him; that was her destiny,' cries Robyn.

'She is fulfilling her destiny, the prophecy, to fight the beast, become the beast, and from the darkness she will see all,' says Annie, cradling Robyn in her arms.

Suddenly from out of the black volcanic mud, a white object flies towards Robyn, landing at her feet, as she picks it up to see a pearl necklace. Annie smiles.

'Remember, I will be watching over you. You are the Inceptor now...'

The bats fly up into the skies, taking Annie, the aurora borealis lighting the way to the heavens, as the RING watch them go.

'What is that?' asks Sam, as Jack pulls Monty up and they all look at the necklace.

The white pearls have crystallized, with thousands of

197

black dots. Charity's ashes, from the fires of hell, immortalised...

'She is still with us,' cries Monty, grabbing the necklace, holding it tight to his chest, as Robyn says:

'The clock is ticking and the world, as we know it, has only twenty-seven years left...'